A WITCH'S DETECTIVE NOVEL

MOURNING HEARTS

KAREN THROWER

World Castle Publishing, LLC
Pensacola, Florida
Copyright © 2025 Karen Thrower
Hardcover ISBN: 9798288609435
Paperback ISBN: 9798891264250
eBook ISBN: 9798891264267
First Edition World Castle Publishing, LLC, July 8, 2025
http://www.worldcastlepublishing.com
Licensing Notes
Cover: Cover Designs by Karen
Editor: Karen Fuller

CHAPTER 1

Ding-dong! My doorbell rang, and I smiled as Detective Richard Moss walked into my apartment. I liked that he did that before he came in, even though he had a key. It was just another thing about him that showed how respectful he was. He was wearing one of his gray suits and the dark purple tie I got him a few weeks ago. Of course, he looked fantastic in it, and that smile on his face made my heart flutter.

"Morning." I put a mug of coffee on the counter for him. I don't know how anyone could drink coffee, let alone drink it black, but he did it without complaint. I suppose that gave him a checkmark in the manly column of life. But he and Nicola thanked me when I finally got a coffee maker for the apartment. I figured it'd save them money from making coffee runs on their way to help me in the mornings.

He leaned down and gave me a long, sweet kiss on my lips. "Morning." His voice was quiet like it always was when he kissed me in the mornings. My stomach still flipped with excitement when he did that, even though it had been six months of kisses. Six months since I woke up in the hospital, my entire right arm immobilized because it had been surgically reattached after a revenant had chopped it off. That was a bad day all around. Not only did I lose my arm, albeit temporarily, but my friends Jackson and Amelia Fell were killed. Leaving me the only witch in Arion. I was just now crawling out of that heavy sadness.

The last few months were the hardest of my adult life. I had never needed to rely on anyone for years, and suddenly, I needed help almost twenty-four hours a day with the most basic of things. Getting dressed, making food, hell, even paying bills on time. But Richard and Nicola really stepped up and helped me. Together, the three of us figured out new ways for me to be more independent while only having one working arm. I couldn't ask for a better friend or boyfriend. "Sleep well?" He gently touched the giant sling that kept my right arm immobilized. I was due to get cleared from it tomorrow, and I was super excited about that. While I could take it off for short periods of time, it wasn't as satisfying as being free of it for good.

"Yeah, it could have been better. I'll probably sleep worse tonight, too excited not to wear this thing anymore." Even though my shoulder was doing better than any surgeon expected, they still insisted I wear the sling, so I obliged. My magic was helping a great deal in my healing. Every day for thirty minutes, I would concentrate on my shoulder or arm and push healing magic through my body. I'd imagine the muscles getting stronger, the tendons being less tight, and it was working. I could move my fingers again, but I could tell they were weak. I could sort of shrug my shoulder, but I didn't do that often, just in case I messed it up. I could even raise my arm in a way that would let me shower and clean myself. Of course, I didn't fight Richard when he wanted to join me and help. I was part-invalid, not stupid.

Richard smiled and took a drink of the black coffee I made him. "Me too." I giggled. God help me, I giggled. We decided that when I no longer had my sling, we could take the next physical step in our relationship. While waiting six months was agony, it was almost over, and I couldn't wait to get him into bed. We had gotten to know each other quite well over the months. What kind of books the other liked to read, and which movies were our favorites. And while I enjoyed every moment with him, we still hadn't gone out much. It was uncomfortable with this awful sling, so we spent most evenings at each other's houses, renting movies or ordering dinner. Sometimes, Nicola would join us, and we'd add in a board game. But now that I'd be free of this giant crutch, well sling, I couldn't wait to show him off around town. And, of course, toss him into bed and do ungodly things to him. From the heat in his eyes, I could tell he felt the same.

"Any idea what Ryan wants?"

I tried hard not to roll my eyes. "No idea." That's why Richard was here so early. Ryan had asked for a meeting with me and Nicola this morning. After the Major apologized for not helping when Jackson and Amelia were killed, his attitude had been a great deal better. I barely remember the apology he gave me in the hospital, but so far, it seemed like he meant every word. But he was still in charge, and I didn't expect the good times to last.

Richard leaned against the counter, the mug in his hands. "Maybe he wants to welcome you back?"

"Pft, doubt that." I laid my left hand on his tie, giving his chest a little rub. "Shall we?"

He finished his coffee and put the mug in the sink. "We shall." He held out his arm, and I took it as we walked from my apartment down to his car. All the officers knew we had been spending a lot of time together. He visited me almost every day while I was in the hospital. I say almost because he didn't exactly escape from that mess intact, either. He had his own healing to do since he got shot in the arm. Thankfully, the bullet didn't do too much damage, and he was back at work six weeks later. But after I was discharged, I couldn't remember a day I didn't see him.

Nicola told me there were rumors flying around the precinct because of the visits. That didn't surprise me one bit. Police officers are some of the nosiest people you'll ever meet. Nicola, of course, knew the truth but would deny it if anyone asked her. Best friend of the year right there. While I totally believed that a man and woman could be just friends, most would rather just tease us. When I mentioned the rumors to Richard, he told everyone who would listen that I was his partner, and no cop let their partner suffer alone. That was something they all understood, and the rumors calmed down a bit. It wasn't like we were denying each other, but we had no idea if they'd even let us date. The last thing I needed to hear was that Ryan had a problem with it, so it was best to keep that bit quiet. Of course it was a small town, so it wouldn't be long before someone saw us on a date. But until then, I wasn't going to worry about it.

We would be careful about not showing affection around the other officers, of course. The sling was huge, and I wasn't allowed to drive while wearing it, so it was a good excuse to let him pick me up in the morning, so there shouldn't be any repercussions for that. He was just a Detective picking up his partner for work. Nothing weird about that.

———

Ten minutes later, we walked into the precinct. A few of the officers smiled and gave me little waves. The ones who were on the scene when my arm got chopped off came over and shook my left hand. It was nice having their respect, but I think I'd rather not have lost an arm in the process. It had been a while since I'd been to the precinct, but I could still do most of my other witchy jobs around town. I didn't need two arms for most of those. Nicola would come to help sometimes, driving me to a client's house and then back home to celebrate a job well done. But the city insisted that I take leave from helping the officers, even though I was a freelancer. I couldn't argue with them on that one. But I'll admit I enjoyed my time away from all the stares and grumbles from the officers that I normally saw.

Richard walked me over to Ryan's office. Nichola was already in there. She was wearing a nice blue skirt with a white silk button-up shirt. Always the consummate professional. I, on the other hand, was wearing a black tank top and leggings. It didn't really occur to me to dress to impress. I was technically still on leave anyway.

"Well, maybe it'll be good news since Nicola is in there." I turned to him, trying desperately to be optimistic. "Sal's for lunch?"

"You're on." His fingers gently ran against mine, where Ryan couldn't see, and walked over to his desk. I turned with a deep breath and walked into the office, head held high.

"Roa, have a seat. How are you?" Ryan scooted up in his chair, and Nicola flashed me one of her perfect smiles and laid her hand on my shoulder as I sat.

"I'm good, getting rid of this thing tomorrow. How are you?" It was odd asking him how he was when in the past, he was usually pissed off at me for something out of my control.

"Doing well, thanks. So, I asked you both here because I have some news, and it affects both of you."

"Please don't tell me I'm fired." I couldn't stop myself. The words just flew out of my mouth. I loved my freelancing gig with the department, and I wasn't sure I could afford my apartment on my witch services alone.

Ryan shook his head with a smile. "No, you're not fired, neither of you. After the unfortunate events last fall—" He always called it that. 'Unfortunate events' not, 'when-I-fucked-up-so-bad-I-got-two-witches-killed-and-you-lost-your-arm-fighting-the-murderer'. Like I said, he was better but hadn't made a total one-eighty. Maybe one-sixty-five? "I managed to convince the city that we needed more preternatural help and that you two deserve more than what we've been giving you."

My eyes went wide. "*You* convinced them?"

"I know," he held up his hand with a smile. "Hard to believe, but I did."

"Are we getting raises?" Nicola leaned forward. She definitely deserved a raise. Hell, who doesn't?

Ryan nodded. "You're both getting raises, and you'll be official employees of the city of Arion, not just freelancers. You'll be given a pension, vacation days, sick days, 401k's, the works. You both deserve this, and I'm sorry I didn't push for it sooner." My jaw dropped, and I looked over at Nicola. She looked the same, and we both laughed and hugged as much as we could.

"It's about damn time." She chuckled and sat back, "I accept."

Ryan smiled. "Good. The other news, because of our need, we'll have two new people joining us in a few days." I sat back, shocked at that. The last thing I expected was for him to hire more help.

"Oh yeah?" He nodded. "Who?"

He pulled up some folders and handed them to us. "The first is another witch to help you, Roa." I couldn't believe what I was hearing and thankfully managed to keep my jaw shut. My eyes, however, gave away my shock as they went wide, and I took the folder from him. "Gwendalyn Savoy is from Connecticut. She's a few years younger than you, but her resume is impressive." I opened the file, and the first thing I saw was her picture. She did look a few years younger, her short hair was purple, and her earrings were moons and stars, I liked her already. She had been working in a magic shop for most of her life but did a lot of free-lancing work in town, helping get rid of entities nobody wanted. I'd hire her.

"Looks good to me." Another witch in town, huzzah! I gave him back the file, desperately holding in my excitement.

Ryan looked over at Nicola. "The other is Dr. Laurette Terraiu. She is an up-and-coming preternatural forensic scientist."

Nicola's eyes went wide. "You're hiring another medical examiner?

He smiled widely, like he knew she was getting what she had asked for Christmas. "We are."

She laughed loudly. "Finally!" She sat back in her chair, a relaxed smile on her face as she looked at her file. "No more digging remains out of werewolf guts?"

Ryan chuckled. "Well, I wouldn't say 'no more.' She will need some help getting her bearings and whatnot, but eventually, all you'll have to deal with are normal people, uh, humans."

"You know, I had no idea this meeting was going to go so well," she put the file back on Ryan's desk and turned to me. "You were afraid of getting fired."

I laughed. "Well, to be fair, Ryan has yelled at me more often than not, so you can understand my hesitation."

He cleared his throat and nodded. "I do hope we can start fresh here, Roa, I'll try to be more understanding."

"I appreciate that a lot, Major." I really did. I just wondered how long it would last. What can I say? It's the pessimist in me.

He handed both of us another manilla folder. "All the paperwork you need to fill out for the city. Roa, you can get someone to help you since writing is a bit hard at the moment.

Get them back to me as soon as you can, and we'll get everything settled."

I took the folder and got to my feet. "Thank you, Major, truly."

"You're welcome, Roa." Nicola snatched up her folder and opened the door for me.

"Bye, Ryan." She waved with the folder, and we walked over to Moss's desk. I couldn't hide the smile on my face if I wanted to. Another witch, I couldn't wait to meet her.

Richard looked up as we got close to his desk and leaned back in his chair. "Oh no, you're both fired, aren't you?" He teased us. "I can tell by your mournful faces." We laughed, and I sat in the chair next to his desk while Nicola leaned against it.

"We're official." She waved her folder.

"You weren't before?" He looked over at me, "Well I knew you weren't, but wait, official?"

I crossed my legs and waved my own folder. "We're employees of the city of Arion and all the perks that come with it."

He smiled, and I saw he almost leaned forward to kiss me but quickly sat back. "That's incredible, congratulations!"

"That's not all," Nicola leaned forward, a big smile on her face. "He hired more help, another witch and another medical examiner who specializes in the preternatural."

"Hey! No more weird shit," he reached out and shook her hand. "Congrats."

She laughed. "Eventually, yes, I'll have to show her around and whatnot, and I'm sure I'll fill in if she's on vacation, but soon." She sighed, and I could see how much it meant to her. I knew that working with things she wasn't familiar with made her nervous. She didn't want to mess something up and let a perp get away or name the wrong killer because she wasn't adept at non-humans. I was glad for her.

I put my folder on his desk. "Care to help me fill it out?"

"Absolutely." He picked up a pen and opened the folder.

"Thanks, I'm sure my handwriting will be atrocious for a while, even with a free hand."

Nicola gently touched my shoulder. "As long as you go to physical therapy, everything will be fine." I groaned. I didn't want to go to physical therapy. I wanted my magic to fix everything. But Nicola insisted it would be good for me, magic or not.

"I know. My first appointment is next Monday."

She gently tapped my head with her folder. "Good. I'll see you later."

"Bye." She walked past me to the stairs that went down to the morgue.

"I'm glad Ryan got you guys what you deserve." Richard was already filling out my paperwork, and I chuckled. He and Nicola knew almost everything about me. Since I had been in the hospital for so long, they helped me take care of mundane things like bills and water plants. And they did it without complaint. I'd have to find a way to thank them both for taking care of me these last six months.

"Me too."

———

Word spread fast about what Ryan had done for us, and the rest of the day was filled with congratulations and gentle yet manly back pats from the other officers. Maybe things would be different now? That night, we sat on my couch while Richard put the Chinese food on the table. I had been craving egg rolls all day, so he bought us a celebratory feast of whatever I wanted from Hot Dynasty. They had the best egg rolls, in my opinion. It wasn't traditional by any means, but it was tasty. I opened the little white bag, and the smell of the egg rolls instantly made my mouth water.

"Thank you, Babe." I scooted up on the couch and carefully loaded my plate with noodles and pork. I reached into the bag and pulled out an egg roll, glad they weren't searing hot and took a bite. I sighed at the taste. It was perfect. Crispy on the outside, and the inside was perfect with cabbage, chicken, and vegetables.

Richard leaned over and kissed my forehead as I chewed. "You're welcome, Sweetheart." My heart flipped as he piled rice and spicy chicken on his plate. "So, I told my parents about you."

I almost choked on my egg roll before I managed to swallow it. "Oh yeah? What'd you say...exactly?" I hadn't had the best track record with parents. They were either scared of me or never learned I existed, so I didn't have a lot of practice with them. Not that I thought his parents' opinion would be enough to influence him to break up with me, but I still couldn't help but hope they liked me. Witch or no.

He smiled. "That I met a beautiful girl in Arion." He leaned toward me. "And she's intelligent," he gave me a kiss. "And thoughtful," another kiss. "And kind."

"Uh-huh," I said against his lips. "Did you tell them what I do for a living?"

He nodded and sat back. "I did. They had questions, of course, but seemed glad I had someone." He took a big bite of rice, but that wasn't going to stop me from asking questions.

"Have you ever dated a witch before?" He shook his head, and spicy chicken joined the rice in his mouth. "What do your parents think about witches?" Magic or not in the world, it could be rare for a human to manifest magic. Sure, humans can do spells and such, but not every magic practitioner could actually touch the magical weave without a spell like I could. It can make mundane people nervous, and nervous people could quickly turn into an angry mob, and I'd like to avoid that.

I waited for him to answer as he took his sweet time chewing that damn bite. "They don't know much about them but know they're regular people. Not anyone to outright fear."

Well, that's good. I sat back and took another bite of egg roll. "They in Oregon?"

"Yeah, they're retired. He was a police officer as well, and mom was a photographer for one of the news stations in town."

Now that impressed me, another woman in a male-dominated field. "Neat. Did you tell your brother and sister about us?"

He swallowed another bite, nodding. "I did. I told them before I told Mom and Dad. Clara is ecstatic, so I think you'll like her. Calvin is more reserved and tends to judge people after he's met them, so he *acknowledged* that I had a girlfriend." I snorted at that. Richard was the oldest of the three, being four years older than the twins. He had shown me pictures of them, and it was hard to believe they were even related. Clara was willowy, and her blonde hair had been dyed black, a real goth girl after my own heart. She was a tattoo artist with her own shop, which made me like her even more. Calvin looked more like Richard, tall with brown hair and green eyes but more slim than muscular. He was a history professor, and Richard warned me that he wasn't a people person, but that was fine with me. I dealt with non-people people all the time.

"Well, I wish I could say I told you about my family, but my cousin doesn't care. Nicola knows about you. That's enough for me."

He smiled. "Good. I like Nicola. You two are good for each

other."

I pulled his arm, and he leaned close. "You're good for me."

"Especially tomorrow night." His voice was low. I could practically hear a growl in it and bit my lower lip.

"Why do we have to wait? I can move my arm." Of course, it was currently in the sling and immobile, but he knew what I meant. "I proved that in the shower, didn't I?" I kissed him softly, waiting to see what he'd do. While we wanted to wait for the big stuff until my arm was free, we did have fun in the shower. It was mostly him washing my hair, even though he didn't have to. I, of course, did my best to run the soap over every part of him when I could.

"You did," I felt his lips against mine as he spoke. "But all we did was clean ourselves. I wasn't about to lift you up and take you against the shower wall." His voice got quieter with every word, and I didn't bother holding back my whine.

"Must you say that in that voice?"

He laughed and kissed my neck. I could smell his dinner on his breath. "I have to do something to keep you interested."

"Trust me, you don't have to do much. It's been a long time since I've had sex."

He chuckled and sat up. "Ending a dry spell, are we?"

"Fuck yes, literally, by the way." He laughed, and I nudged his knee with my foot. "How long has it been for you?"

He swallowed his bite. "Um, eight months? I was still in Oregon."

"That's not horrible, better than mine." I finished my egg roll and grabbed the second one.

"What's yours?" He opened his beer and took a drink. I liked the way beer smelled, but not the taste, so all the beer in my fridge had been put there by him.

I took a bite. "Two years," I said around the mouthwatering egg roll.

He almost choked on his drink. "Two years? You haven't been with anyone in two years?"

I shook my head and slurped up some noodles. "Nope. You get used to it."

He sighed and shook his head. "Hell of a thing to get used to." He put his fork down and turned to me. "Don't tell me you never gave yourself pleasure."

My eyes went wide, and I quickly swallowed my bite. "You don't get to know that." I booped his nose, and he smiled a new kind of smile. One I had never seen before. It was wicked almost as he slowly leaned forward, pressing me against the couch behind me.

"Why not?" He practically breathed it.

I chuckled. "You're withholding from me. I can do it to you, too," I whispered against his cheek. He sighed as he kissed my neck. I reached around with my left hand and held him there as his lips, teeth, and tongue made tingles spread along my body. He moved up my neck and kissed my lips, his teeth pulling my bottom lip between his. I pressed against him, but a shock of pain down my arm made me gasp, and he quickly sat up.

"Are you okay?" His hand went to my shoulder. "I'm sorry I didn't mean to hurt you." That lovely low voice full of heat and tease was gone as he searched for whatever caused me discomfort.

I shook my head. "You didn't, you're fine." I sat up, annoyed that my arm had decided right then to hurt. "The doctor said that as I gained the feeling back in my arm, I'd get those shocks of pain. It wasn't you." He was with me when the doctor said that, so hopefully, he would believe me. I laid a hand on his cheek. "Remember?"

He nodded and sighed, almost relieved. "I do." He ran his thumb along my cheek. "Hopefully, those won't last long."

"Hopefully not." I took a drink of my pop, eyeing him out of the corner of my eye. If he wouldn't give me what I wanted, maybe he would at least stay over. "You know, you can stay over if you want. We can just sleep." He had a drawer and part of the closet for a few suits for just such an occasion.

He smiled then looked over at me. "I'd like that."

CHAPTER 2

My alarm went off at seven am, and when I opened my eyes, I couldn't help but smile. Richard's arm was around my waist, and he was pressed against my back. It was the first time he had stayed over, and it was wonderful. I got an eyeful of him in his boxer briefs. His chest had a little tuft of dark hair in the middle that I ran my fingers through as we laid in bed and talked. He didn't snore, at least from what I heard, and I fell asleep in his arms. I reached over and silenced my alarm.

"Morning," he grumbled, sounding tired as he stretched.

I couldn't stop my chuckle. "Not a morning person?"

"Never trust a morning person." I laughed and turned to him as he wrapped his arms around me again. "Today's the day."

"I can't wait to be free of this thing." He kissed my forehead and slid out of bed. I couldn't help but enjoy the view of him in his boxer briefs. The muscles of his thighs looked powerful, and he had those lovely hip dips.

He chuckled, and it woke me from my reverie. "Enjoying the view?"

"Mm-hmm." I stretched, and the blanket fell away from me. I was wearing an oversized t-shirt but not so big that my boobs were going to flop out like they do in a tank top. Nothing special at all, but he still smiled.

"Me too."

———

Two hours later, we were at the surgeon's office, and I was sitting on an exam table. My arm was free from the hefty sling and was being manipulated and tested by the surgeon to make sure I didn't need it anymore. I pushed against his hand a million different ways and flexed my fingers and elbow, and moved my arm every way I could think of to show him it was fine. My shoulder was numb around the scars, and he said I may or may not get feeling back there, but it was definitely coming back down my arm, hence the random shooting pains.

I could move my arm and pick up things that were less than five pounds. That was from my magic. But the skin and most of the nerves still didn't have a lot of sensation. I hoped that some of the physical therapy would help with that. Nicola said it was like the nerves had to relearn where to make the connection, and the therapy would do that. It was weird being able to move my arm but not feel most of it. I glanced over at my shoulder. The scar was thick and pink and was dotted with little pink scars all the way around it. If I colored them in and played connect the dots, I'd make a decent Frankenstein costume for Halloween.

"All right, Ms. Roa, you're much farther along than most people who have had a limb reattached. I was told you did a lot of healing magic on it?"

"Yes." I lowered my arm. "No more sling, right?"

"Nope, no more sling, but—" he reached behind him in a drawer and pulled out a smaller sling that was just something for my arm to lay in. "If your arm gets tired, or your shoulder starts hurting, wear this, and it should help. If it gets tired, let it rest. Don't use your magic to heal everything, okay?" I nodded. "You're further along but not a hundred percent yet. You start physical therapy next week, right?"

"Yes." I took the sling and immediately gave it to Richard.

He had a little smirk on his face.

"Good. I want to see you in two months, see how much you've progressed. Don't overdo it, no hand-to-hand combat or anything," he said as he typed something into my file.

I snapped my fingers. "Oh, darn, there goes my karate tournament." The doctor looked up, concerned, but Richard laughed and put a hand on my shoulder.

"She's joking."

I nodded, and the doc visibly calmed down. "Oh, good. You'd be surprised at how many people don't listen to our advice and get hurt all over again."

That honestly didn't surprise me. "I think if my arm gets chopped off a second time, I'm just gonna leave it off. Clearly, the universe is telling me something."

He patted my shoulder, but I didn't feel much. "Hopefully, that won't happen. You take care now, all right?" He shook my hand, and I could feel the muscle difference in it, but it was better than a limp handshake. He left us alone, and Richard helped me down from the table. I could get down myself, but I'd never turn down an occasion where he had his hands on me.

I put my light sweater on by myself for the first time in months, and I smiled. "How shall we celebrate?"

He put his hand on my back as we walked back to the front desk. "Well, I think first we need to go to work."

My smile quickly disappeared. "Boo."

He laughed. "You can go around showing off your new arm."

That did appeal to me. "True."

"Then tonight I'll order dinner," he put an arm around me. "We'll eat, and then, who knows, maybe fall asleep watching TV?" I snorted and made my appointment at the receptionist, and we walked to the parking garage.

"We can fall asleep watching TV after I screw your brains out."

His laughter echoed in the parking garage. "Yes, ma'am."

———

Richard parked in the underground parking lot at work, and we walked into the morgue.

"Nicola!" I yelled. It was normally super quiet in the morgue, so I hoped I didn't scare her.

"Yes?" I heard her yell from where her desk was around the corner.

"Guess what?" We walked around the corner, and she looked up and smiled.

"How's it feel?" We stopped at her desk, and I gave her the full show, moving my arm up and down and making a slow circle.

"So far so good. He gave me a sling if it starts hurting or anything. Hopefully, it won't, I'm sick of those things."

She stood and gave me a hug. "I'm so glad you're doing better. I can't tell you how awful it was seeing you all laid up in hospital." Being the only medical examiner in town, she was at the mansion when everyone finally showed up. I know it must have been hard on her, seeing Jackson and Amelia like that. Then me. She told me Ryan ran out of the mansion with me in his arms, my bleeding stump pressed to his chest, yelling for a medic. I didn't remember any of it. But the way he'd been acting lately, it sure seemed like he was scared at the time and glad I pulled through.

"I'm sorry to put you through that, but I'm glad you were there for me." I took her hand and Richard's hand, "Both of you. I don't know what I would do without you." Richard dared a kiss on my head.

"Anytime luv." She picked up her file with her papers for the city and held it up. "Got yours ready?"

Richard nodded. "They're on my desk."

"Well, let's go hand them in before Ryan changes his mind." I smiled as I took her arm and we rode the elevator up to the bullpen. I got my folder off Richard's desk, and we walked to Ryan's office. I knocked with my right hand and could feel the weak muscles in my wrists. That was going to have to change.

He looked up and smiled. "All done?" We walked in and handed him our paperwork. "Excellent. Roa, nice to see you back in one piece."

"Nice to be in one piece." A picture of him covered in my blood flashed in my mind, but I had no idea if it was a memory or my mind trying to put together what Nicola told me. Real or not, it was disturbing to see, and I reached down and grasped Nicola's hand. I felt her give me a little squeeze, and I felt better. Ryan didn't seem to notice as he was turned away from us, putting the folders in a basket behind his desk.

"I'll get these turned in. Welcome to the team. Oh, Roa," he turned back around. "Go check by Moss's desk. I think there's something for you."

I looked up at Nicola, and she shrugged. "All right." I didn't see anything on the way over to his office, but then again, I wasn't looking for anything in particular.

"Thank you, Major." Nicola let go of my hand and took my arm as we walked back to Moss's desk. He was standing by his chair with a smile on his face. I noticed there was a wall of officers behind him. They were all smiling.

"All set?" He asked and leaned against his desk.

"Yep."

"Good. Surprise." The officers moved, and I saw a desk behind his, and my name was on a nameplate on it.

I gasped and pointed at it. "Where did that come from?"

"We carried it over while you were in Ryan's office," Hyde said with a smile. Being a consultant, I never had a desk before. I always worked from home, or Howard let me sit at his desk. It felt nice that I was being included this way.

Richard stood next to me. "Now that you're official, Ryan thought you might need a desk by me." One of the officers, Derrick, I think his name was, pulled out my chair for me. I looked back at Nicola, and she nodded. So, I took a seat, and one by one, the officers came and shook my hand or patted my shoulder. They welcomed me back and said they were glad I was on the mend. It was odd, feeling this gratitude from them after years of mean stares and ignoring me. I suppose seeing me sans-arm scared them.

I swiveled to Richard. The way our desks were situated, our backs faced each other, but we had a little space between them, so if we needed to huddle, we could.

"I could get used to this."

Richard patted my shoulder. "I certainly hope you do."

A young man came walking up and put a computer on my desk. "Hi, I'm Walker, I'll get your computer set up." I had seen his name on emails and knew he was in IT. He was in his twenties, wearing a short-sleeved button-up shirt, and had a huge keyring attached to his belt.

"Thanks." I held out my hand, and he gave it a quick shake. That little tingle of magic hit my hand, and I knew he was a shifter of some kind. But I wasn't really in the shifter circles, so I couldn't tell what kind off the top of my head. You'd think I would be more familiar with the shifters in town, but I assumed they wouldn't want a witch hanging around. But maybe I was wrong, and the town's impression of me had rubbed off on me more than I realized.

———

That night, Richard drove us to his place. He had given me a drawer and space in his closet for things a month prior, so I wasn't worried about stopping by my apartment. I had a toothbrush, a brush, clothes, anything I needed that wasn't witchy related. I loved Richard's house. It was an adorable little two-room cape-cod style house like they all were on this street. He mowed the lawn, but he wasn't much of a gardener, so he told me when I was able to, I could have free reign of the yard. I gave him an enthusiastic kiss for that. Me living that apartment life, I had no garden, so his giving me permission to plant what I wanted was an exciting prospect. I already had plans for every inch of his yard, flowers, and bushes, maybe a tree in the front. The back would be covered in herbs and anything I could grow for my magic. Now, I just needed my arm to get stronger.

He ordered Italian from Intermezzo's, and we ate at the dining room table like normal people. That was something I lacked in my apartment. Not because there wasn't room. I just didn't see the need when it was just me there. When we ate enough that we were full but not busting, we sat on the couch and talked. Our fingers trailing over bits of skin, getting used to one another with my now free arm. When I finally pulled him to me, he didn't hesitate as he leaned back, holding me against him as I kissed his lips, his cheeks, and his neck. I wanted to kiss every inch of him.

His hands slid under my shirt, his fingers kneading gently along my ribs. His thumbs rubbed little circles on my skin, and they were getting higher and higher. I swore I felt him brush the underside of my breast when his phone rang.

"Mother fu —" I glanced at the phone and saw it was Ryan. "You have got to be kidding me." Thankfully, he could reach it from where I had him trapped on the couch because I did not want to move.

He snickered a moment before answering. "Detective Moss."

We were so close I could hear Ryan on his phone. "*Moss, it's Ryan. We have someone in custody, and we're hoping you can bring Roa in and help them, uh, regain their mind?*"

"Regain their mind?" He looked at me, and I nodded before laying my head back on his chest. "I'm sure she can do something about that. What did they do?"

"At the moment, we're charging them with first-degree murder. He killed his girlfriend, but he's saying a faerie told him to do it." I lifted my head at that. It had been a while since someone had used the old 'a faerie told me to do it' excuse. I could tell from his tone Ryan didn't believe the guy. But Moss was right. I could help.

"All right, we'll be right there." He hung up, and we looked at each other. "Maybe it won't take long?" He suggested. I was glad one of us was being optimistic because I sure wasn't going to be.

"Maybe." I gave him one more lingering kiss. "Can we stop by my apartment first? I want to pick up some things I might need."

"Absolutely."

———

Ten minutes later, we were finally on our way to the station, with all my special baubles in my pocket. The sun had been down at least an hour now, and the lights zoomed past us, lighting up the inside of the car with that dull yellow light all highways had.

I leaned forward and moved the vent from blowing right on my leg. "Been a while since someone blamed a fae for making them kill someone."

"Has it?"

I nodded and sat back. "Few years at least. Last one was a guy who wanted a divorce, but his wife wouldn't grant it without trying therapy first. When they found her body on the baseball field, they immediately brought him in because you know it's the spouse ninety-nine percent of the time."

He scoffed. "Right."

"He said he wanted a divorce because he met someone. She was fae and told him she only wanted him and no one else. But he was dumb and gave us her real name, so I summoned her. She was horrified at what he had done. Said she never said that and would never tell anyone to murder their significant other. And you know how fae can't lie."

He shook his head. "You'd think most people would know that."

I shrugged and laid my hand on his thigh. "No one said criminals are smart."

He reached down and rubbed my hand. "I rather think they're not." I chuckled and watched the lights zoom by, crossing my fingers that this wouldn't take long.

———

I followed Richard to the interrogation rooms on the second floor. We walked inside number three and saw through the two-way mirror a man sitting at the table, covered in blood, tears streaming down his face. He didn't look like he was enthralled, but I suppose anything was possible. Hyde shook

Richard's hand, and he gave me a nod.

"This is Marcus Wind. His neighbors called 911 because they heard screaming. When we got there, we could see through the window that he was cradling the body of a woman, so we forced entry. He didn't seem to notice us as we ran in and got her away from him, but it was too late. There was a large kitchen knife sticking out of her chest." He set some crime scene pictures down on the table, and I riffled through them. The poor girl didn't stand a chance. The knife went right into her heart, so there was blood everywhere. The victim and suspect both looked to be in their early twenties. Her bio paper said she was a kindergarten teacher. Damn it, those poor kids.

"How long were they together?" I moved aside so Richard could look at them.

"Three years. When we asked what happened, he said he did it, that he killed her. But that a faerie made him do it so they could be together."

I crossed my arms and looked back at the suspect. "Hmm."

Hyde leaned against the table. "Know much about faeries, Roa?"

"Yeah, but I'm unsure his story about being enthralled is holding up." I looked up at Hyde. "Can we talk to him?"

He nodded and motioned to the door. "Be my guest." I motioned for Richard to follow me, and we walked into the other room. The smell of blood hit my nose first, and my mind flashed back to the day I lost my arm. The interrogation room was replaced with the library in the mansion, and I saw my arm on the floor. I shook my head to get rid of the vision and took a calming breath, willing my nervous heart to calm down. Thankfully, Richard noticed my hesitation and took point.

"Mr. Wind, I'm Detective Moss. This is my partner, Lily

Roa. We have some questions for you." He sat down across from Marcus, and thankfully, by then, everything was back to normal. No more severed arm or bloody floor. I paced behind Richard, letting my magic see if it could tell me anything. I slid my hand into my pocket and held the onyx stone in my hand and cast a spell. I wanted to see if there was any fae magic in the room. If there was, the stone would vibrate in my hand.

All magic can leave traces. No matter how good you are at covering your tracks, there's always something there. Fae magic was strong and connected to the earth. Usually, when I detected it, I smelled dirt and flowers, but at that moment, all I smelled was blood. One thing was for certain, this man was not under any compulsion or magic of any kind. Those who are under the influence of any kind of charm, be it fae or human or any other creature, had a certain glow about them. No matter what they were told to do, love, kill, hide, they had that same glow that I just didn't see on him. That and the still stone in my hand made me wonder why he thought he could get away with blaming a fae for this.

"Marcus, how long were you and the victim dating?" I asked him, still pacing. I wanted to see how he did with a bunch of quick questions in a row.

"Three years."

"And how long had you known this fae?"

"Two months."

"What do you do for work?"

"I'm a file clerk."

"What's the fae's name?"

"Buttercup."

"What color hair does Buttercup have?"

"Blonde."

"Where did you meet Buttercup?"

"At the park."

"When did you decide to kill your girlfriend?"

"Tonight." His eyes went wide, and I stopped pacing to face him. "I mean, Buttercup told me to do it tonight."

"Uh-huh," I pulled out the onyx stone and walked closer to him. "See this? It reacts to fae magic, and," I put it close to his face, and it did nothing. "There's no fae magic around you. You are not nor have ever been under any kind of fae compulsion." I pocketed the stone and crossed my arms. "So, you want to try again?" He looked between me and Richard. I could see the wheels turning in his head, trying to come up with an excuse.

"I...I don't know. Maybe she took it off? I swear she told me to do it!" His eyes were wild and wide as he tried to get Richard to see his side, but I knew it wouldn't work.

I walked behind Richard in case he decided to get grabby. "If any self-respecting fae female wanted a man who already had a lover, she wouldn't ask him to kill his love. She'd ask her to join them. Fae prize love above most things. You should have done your homework better, Marcus." Richard sat back, crossing his own arms as he stared at the suspect.

Marcus's eyes darkened as the tears stopped, and he stared at me. "Fucking witch bitch," he growled.

But I just smiled and made sure he heard my sweet, happy tone. "Have fun in prison."

Hyde came in and lifted the man to his feet and took him away.

"That was well done." Richard got to his feet and shook my hand, a proud smile on his face.

"Do we need to fill out paperwork, or can we leave?"

He sighed, and I knew that sigh, that was a disappointed

sigh. "Yes, there's paperwork."

I grumbled and walked from the room. "Poor woman, why can't men just vagina up and break up with a girl instead of killing her like a coward."

He snickered behind me. "Did you just say vagina up?"

"I most certainly did," I said, not turning around. "Those things take a beating." He laughed as he sat at his desk, and I sat at mine and turned to face him as he pulled up the pages he needed on his computer. "Gotta love bureaucracy."

"Oh yeah." He turned and winked at me, and I smiled, hoping no one saw. My arms broke out in goosebumps, and I turned to see Will sitting on my desk, a big smile on his face. I hadn't seen him in months, and I missed him. He had to have broken a few hearts when he was alive. He was too good-looking not to have. His dark blonde hair was wavy and hung down to his neck. He had a strong jaw and pretty blue eyes.

"Look atcha now, my bonny lass has her own desk!" He patted it but stayed sitting on it.

I smiled and gave the desk a pat. "I know, isn't it great?"

My ear twitched as Richard's chair squeaked behind me. "Has Will graced us with his presence?" I turned and fought not to bite my lip at how handsome the smile on Richard's face made him.

"He has."

"Hello, Will," he said as he turned back to his desk.

"Evening Detective." Will gave him a little nod even though he couldn't see it.

"He said, 'Evening Detective.'" I heard Richard chuckle as he started typing. Richard had been a little go-to between us over the last few months. I told him to write down what happened to me so Will could read it and not start a ruckus as to why I hadn't been there. He'd also write down when I'd ask the ghost not to bug Nicola because she had a rough night. So far, it seemed to work. The handsome ghost rolled on his back and spread his arms out across my desk. Thankfully, he didn't knock anything off.

"I'm glad you're back, my bonny lass, I missed ya. Moss said you was hurt but not how bad." His usual playful smile disappeared as he sat back up. "I was worried about ya." I had never seen him be serious. Well, he was sort of serious last fall when he was tracking the spell that the Order had put in the precinct. But never like he was now.

"I was. A revenant cut my arm off." I pulled the neck of my shirt down and showed him my scar. His eyes went wide as he leaned toward me. A few things on my desk shook as he reached out for my shoulder. His fingers were cold as they ran along my scar, but he was gentle. Will didn't touch me often, probably because I saw him coming, so it wasn't as funny. But when he did, it was always for a good reason. The last time was a few years ago when my last boyfriend broke up with me. I was crying down in the morgue, waiting for Nicola, when he popped up and wiped my tears away without a word.

"Aw Hen," he rarely called me that. It was something akin to sweetheart. "That looks painful."

I looked back at my scar. "Honestly, I didn't feel much. I think it was adrenaline and being in shock. The doctors were good at managing my pain, too. I only had a few bad days." I never thought I'd feel pain worse than cramps, but a healing limb reattachment, that knocked me on my ass a few times. Thankfully, Nicola was able to get my pain meds quicker those days. Will's eyes moved between my shoulder and my eyes. There was something in them I hadn't ever seen before. It almost looked like longing.

"You talking to the ghost Roa?" Hyde's voice broke my concentration, and I looked over at him. He was sitting in the chair next to Richard's desk.

"Yeah, I hadn't seen him in a while." I pulled my shirt back over my shoulder. "He wanted to know why I'd been gone, so I showed him my scar." Will got off my desk and stood next to me. His arms crossed like he was waiting for Hyde to do something rude.

"What's the ghost's name?"

I looked up at Will, who shrugged. "It's William McKay. He goes by Will. Or at least that's what I call him." He walked over to Hyde and tickled his cheek, but the officer just brushed the sensation away as if it were a stray hair or something. I chuckled and shook my head.

"Well, nice to meet you, Will," Hyde said to thin air, and Will laughed.

"I think he's the first cop that's said that. Tell him it's nice to meet him as well."

I smiled and looked back at Hyde. "He said, 'It's nice to meet you as well.'"

Will reached down and touched my shoulder. "I'll see you later, Hen."

"Uh, be cool, huh? Ryan's actually being nice, and I want it to last."

He sighed, clearly irritated, I asked. "For you, my bonny Hen, I will." He sank through the floor, and I felt bad for whoever was in the morgue.

"Do you talk to ghosts often?" Hyde asked.

"Not every day, but if I'm all desk official now, I probably will. I'm sure he'll like that. Maybe it'll keep him better behaved?"

He turned to Richard, who had been typing away as we talked. "How do you feel about having a partner who talks to dead guys?"

I could see the corner of his mouth tilt in a smile. "I love it. It's another aspect to a case that I normally wouldn't have. And you get used to it." He said with a shrug.

"You really do." I agreed.

"So you're like, friends with him?" It felt like he had a million questions but wasn't sure which ones were going to offend me. Honestly, it was hard to offend me. The more questions, the better.

"I think so, as much as one can be friends with a dead guy."

"Least he's good looking, right?" Richard teased me, and I kicked the back of his chair.

"You are going to get me in trouble." He laughed, and I shook my head.

Hyde tried to hide his smile but failed miserably. "He's good looking?"

"He doesn't look like a flesh rotting zombie or something. He looks like he did in life. And *yes*, he's handsome, so what? He knows he's handsome too, the little shit."

Hyde finally laughed, and it felt like he was relaxing. "I always thought he was just a menace."

"Well, he can be. But if you want a little tip, put butterscotch on your desk. He loves the smell of it, so he won't knock anything off your desk."

"Butterscotch, really?" I nodded. "I'll give it a try, thanks."

"No problem." I sat back and practiced moving my elbow. "So, did our guy finally confess for really reals?"

Hyde nodded. "Really reals, said there was no faerie and

was jealous of all the time she spent doing her job instead of with him." He shook his head and sighed. "What a waste."

"Ugh, asshole."

"Okay, Ms. Roa," Richard finished typing and turned to us. "I can email you the report, and you can fill out all the magical stuff."

"Oh, yeah, you could if I had set up my email earlier." I grimaced at my first official failure. I didn't think I'd need it so fast!

He snickered. "I see. You can sit here if you want." Richard got up from his chair, so I moved over and sat in it. It was warm and comfy.

"Thank you. I'll get it set up tomorrow, I promise." It had been a while since I typed so much, but I was determined to do it properly and not just with my pointer fingers. But after two sentences, my wrist was sore. "Damn it." I rubbed my wrist and sat back.

"You want me to type out what you say instead?" I felt Richard's hand on my right shoulder.

"No, no, I gotta get all my muscles back to where they were. I'll just type slower."

He patted my left shoulder. "Okay, if you need to stop, let me know."

"I will."

"Nah, don't worry about her, Moss," Hyde gave my back a pat as he got to his feet, "Roa's got this."

"Damn right, I do."

———

It was eleven when we finally got back to Richard's house, and I could barely keep my eyes open. Thankfully, the ibuprofen I took at the station helped with my wrist. I was so damn slow typing. Getting home this late was all my fault. Well, to be completely honest, it was the guy who killed his girlfriend, but my slow ass didn't help.

"Asshole ruining our night," I grumbled, and belly flopped onto his bed, fully clothed. I breathed in deep, his bed smelled like his cologne, and I loved that spicy, orange smell.

"I know." He flopped down next to me, and I felt his hand on my back. "I don't even want to shower."

"Morning shower." I managed to turn and sit up and kicked my shoes off. He did the same. "You know we're not that old. We shouldn't be this tired."

"Yet we are." He pulled his shirt off and undid his belt. "Murder takes it out of you, no matter what side you're on."

"Suppose so." I went to my drawer and pulled out a big t-shirt. "Need in the bathroom?"

"Naw, you go." He waved at me as his pants fell to the floor. I giggled as he fell back to the bed and shut the door behind me. I quickly changed and brushed my teeth and hair. When I walked back into the bedroom, he was fast asleep on the bed, not even under the covers. I turned the light off on the side table and crawled onto the bed and snuggled against him.

His arms wrapped around me and held me close. "Night, Lily," he mumbled.

"Night."

"Love you." I smiled against his chest, and I wondered if he'd remember saying that in the morning.

"Love you."

CHAPTER 3

My alarm went off, and I opened my eyes. It was the second morning I woke with Richard's arms around me, and I smiled. I reached out and silenced my phone as he stretched and kissed my right shoulder. It had snuck its way out of my t-shirt in the night. I could feel his kiss, but not where I expected it to be. He kissed the back of my shoulder, but I felt it closer to my armpit. It was odd. At least I didn't feel it on my ass or some other weird place. Not that they took any skin from my ass, but the thought made me chuckle.

I snuggled my back up against his front. "Morning." I turned my head and watched him kiss along the fat, pink scar that went around my entire arm. I chuckled. "What are you doing?"

"I'm sure you know," he kissed my neck as his hand snuck under my shirt. "When I'm at the station late at night, I come in late the next morning. You can do that, too." I felt his hand spread out on my bare stomach.

"I can, huh?"

"Mm-hmm." His hand moved to my hip and ran down my thigh. I shifted, and he took the hint and ran his hand on the inside of my leg. I sighed and moved against him, feeling how hard he was. He moaned and squeezed my thigh. "Can I touch you?" He whispered in my ear.

"I'm going to be mad if you don't." He laughed as he kissed my neck, and I felt his fingers slide between my legs, and

I gasped as that electric pleasure filled me when he ran his finger around my clit. He sighed as I reached down and laid my hand over his, feeling how his finger was giving me pleasure. I held him still and moved against him like he was a living toy, and he chuckled.

"Do whatever you need to do, Sweetheart," he said in that low voice that always turned me on. "I'm here for you."

"Are you?"

I turned, and he had that sexy smirk on his lips. "Whatever you want."

"I want your face between my legs." His smirk got wider as he removed his finger and slid down the bed, his eyes burning into mine.

"I've been waiting for you to say that." He pulled my underwear down and threw them somewhere in the room, then spread my legs. I bit my lower lip and watched as he licked straight up my middle. I couldn't help but throw my head back and moan at the sensation as his tongue licked where his finger once was. I reached down and buried my fingers in his thick, soft hair. At first, he was slow, learning what I liked, then it was like an onslaught of my senses as he slowly sucked while he slid a finger inside me. He hit a spot, and I couldn't stop my hips as they moved with him.

I could feel an orgasm building. My poor body hadn't had one from someone else in two years, so I suppose I could understand its urgency, so I relaxed and let it happen. My hands flew up by my head, and I didn't hold back as my orgasm broke inside me like a dam. I cried out as my body throbbed with pleasure, and after one more lick, he crawled up my body. I watched as he put his finger in his mouth and licked me off his skin. "You taste how I thought you would."

I laughed. "Do I?" I reached between us and palmed the hardness I found.

He moaned and laid his forehead on mine. His phone rang, but he ignored it. "I'm in the shower."

"So am I." I squeezed him, and he moaned into the crick of my neck, and my body responded, eager to feel him in me. But whoever it was didn't leave a message, they called again.

"Mother fuc—" he reached over, and resignation filled his eyes as he answered. "Yeah." He put a finger to his lips, which was fine. I'd be quiet. But I was still holding a particularly sensitive piece of his body in my hand and gave it a little squeeze. He squeezed his eyes shut as he bit his lower lip. I could hear Hyde on the other end.

"Sorry to wake you. We've had another murder where they're blaming a faerie."

"I see," his voice was strained as I held him. I didn't move my hand. I just kept that pressure up.

"Can you call Roa and come down to the station? Maybe she can do what she did with Wind, and we can wrap this up quickly."

"Yep, no problem. Lemme shower." He spoke in quick, short sentences because that's all he could get out.

"Okay, see you two in a bit."

He hung up and tossed his phone onto a pile of clothes. "You wicked little witch." His fingers tickled my sides, and I couldn't stop the screech that came out of my mouth, especially since he rolled me on top of him. He wrapped his arms around me, and I laid my head on his chest. "I'm sorry I started something we can't finish right now." He ran his hand over my hair.

"What do you mean?" I looked up, and he still had that heat in his eyes, but there was also something else. It looked like regret.

"I thought we'd have time this morning, otherwise I wouldn't have done that."

I ran my fingers through the hair on his forehead. "I don't mind what you did. It was amazing."

He smiled and kissed my forehead. "I know, it was, and I'm glad we had a little fun. But I want to take *hours* with you, Roa."

The corner of my mouth tilted in a smirk. "Hours, you say?"

"Hours. I didn't want our first time to be rushed because we had to get somewhere. I wanted to take the time and get to know every inch of you." I smiled. "And now we can't."

"You wanted to take your time with me?" He nodded. It was the most romantic thing I'd heard. It would be nice to be tangled up in bed for hours, just getting to know each other's bodies. "I'm up for that. I want our first time to be special, too."

He ran his hand through my hair and kissed my forehead. "Then it will be."

———

An hour later, we were in the same room we were in the night before. Looking at another young man in the interrogation room, but he wasn't crying like Wind had been. He was just staring at the table, his fingers laced together. If he was faking being enthralled, he was doing an excellent job.

Hyde put a file of pictures on the table. "Jordan Glass, age twenty-four, killed his girlfriend early this morning by strangling her." I opened the file and perused the pictures. The young woman was in bed on her back. I could see pinprick bruising on her face, and her eyes were bloodshot, which was consistent with strangulation. Poor thing. "He called 911 and said he killed his girlfriend. When we got there, he was sitting on the porch. She was inside on the bed."

"Did he say why he did it?" Richard started rifling through the pictures.

"He said there was a faerie in the house, and it told him to kill her." I waited for him to continue, but he didn't.

"That's it?"

He nodded and shrugged. "That's it."

"Does Glass know Wind?" Richard crossed his arms and looked at the suspect.

"So far, we haven't come up with any connections, but that doesn't mean there aren't any."

"Hmm, well, good thing I still have my trusty rock." I turned to Richard. "Let's go say hi." He nodded, and we walked into the room. He took the chair across from the suspect while I paced again. I reached up and held the crystal around my neck and cast a little spell to see enchantments and held in my gasp. Glass was glowing. I walked closer and breathed in deep. I could smell his cologne, but no wind, no dirt or flowers. Whoever did this to him was no fae.

"Mr. Glass, my name is Detective Moss. This is my partner, Lily Roa. Can you tell me what happened?"

His eyes slowly moved from his hands and up to Moss. "The fae...said to kill her." The lack of emotion in his voice and the glowy skin confirmed, without a doubt, someone had enthralled him. "I had to."

"Can you tell us about the fae in the room?" Props to Richard for asking it the right way.

He seemed to think for a moment. "Beautiful, transcendent, powerful."

"Any more adjectives?" I stood behind Richard, my arms crossed.

His eyes looked up at me and blinked a few times. "Huh?" He was bad. I had to dispel whatever was on him.

I leaned down behind Ricard and whispered. "This guy is definitely enthralled. Can I dispel it?"

"Yeah, go ahead." I put my hands together, palm to palm, and my magic bloomed from me and filled the entire room. I like to think it's like plugging in a lamp. Palm to palm was like putting a plug into a wall. You did that, and boom, light. Or, in my case, magic. I put my right hand on the table, and my magic flowed around him. I could feel the spell on him, but my arm decided that was the best time for one of those lightning pains.

I gasped and, held my arm against me, and walked behind Richard. "What's wrong?" He stood and held my arm, but this pain seemed to want to linger. Wave after wave of electrical pain raced down my arm. I couldn't concentrate, and my magic receded back into me.

"I apologize, just one of those healing pains." I caught my breath and saw the suspect was looking at my arm.

Suddenly, I broke out in goosebumps and watched Will walk in the room. "Let me help ya, Hen."

He reached for my arm. "What are you gonna do?" But he didn't answer. He just wrapped his ghostly fingers around the upper part of my arm. His fingers were cold like they were the night before, and somehow, the pain melted away, and I was able to relax. "How'd you do that?" But he just smiled and walked away.

"What happened?" Richard whispered to me.

"Will made the pain go away." I took a deep, cleansing breath before turning back to the suspect and called up my magic once again, and quickly enveloped him in it before the pain could come back. "*Desisto*," I said quietly and willed the spell on him to end for his mind to be his own once again. The bright light he was putting off dimmed to nothing, and he shook his head. I recalled my magic and sighed. "How do you feel?"

He looked around the room. Confusion was evident in his eyes. "Where am I?" I wasn't surprised he didn't know where he was. Coming out of a compulsion can come with memory loss. It could come back with some help, unfortunately, that might include looking at pictures of his dead girlfriend. I felt sorry for him.

Richard walked over and stood next to me. "Arion police station. Do you remember what happened?" His eyes were wide, but I could tell he was trying to remember.

"No, last thing I remember was going to bed. Why am I here? How did I get here?" He looked between us, and Richard motioned to the glass. We tried to keep the man calm before the counselor walked in. Her name was Gloria, and I had to talk to her to be cleared for duty after my arm. She was nice, totally mundane, but nice. Her dark hair was always in a bun behind her head, and she wore ballet slippers, probably because she was tall and didn't want to intimidate any of the officers. I never understood that if I were almost six feet, I'd wear heels every day. Her main duty was explaining to humans how they were used by something to commit a crime. It was a rough job, but she seemed suited for it. We walked into the other room and watched as she sat across from the suspect and told him why he was there.

At first, he didn't believe her. He said he loved his girlfriend, and he'd never hurt her. Then Hyde walked in and showed him the pictures. He practically went catatonic before he started crying. He had remembered. We left him alone with Gloria for a bit. He wouldn't be answering any questions while crying like that. Me, Richard, and Hyde stood in the other room, keeping an eye on the both of them through the mirror.

"So, you said he was definitely enthralled?" Hyde crossed his arms as he turned to me.

"Yeah, he was all glowy and everything. Did you notice how he spoke before I dispelled him?" I gave Richard's foot a little tap with my own.

"He was completely out of it," he said, watching the poor man sob in the room.

"What are the odds that one guy fakes a fae influence and the other is legit?" Hyde gathered up the pictures and put them in the folder.

"Weirder things have happened." I sat at the table and started moving my arm around.

"Does it hurt?" Hyde's eyebrows went up, showing genuine curiosity.

I shook my head. "Not anymore."

"It doesn't usually last that long, does it?" Richard looked at me. I could tell he was worried because he was right. That was the first time the pain didn't immediately go away.

"No, it doesn't. Maybe it means I'm getting more feeling back quicker?"

"That'd be nice." We waited until Glass calmed down, and Gloria left the room and came to tell us what he said.

"He says he remembers killing her but didn't want to and that he loved her."

We all nodded. "Thanks, Gloria." She walked away with a little smile before Richard and I went back in the room. The suspect's demeanor had taken a one-eighty. He was visibly upset, his eyes were red from crying, and his shoulders were slumped.

"Mr. Glass, do you feel up to answering some questions?" Richard took the seat across from him once again.

"Yeah, sure, I'll do my best," he said quietly as he wiped his wet cheeks.

"What's the last thing you remember before you saw the fae?"

He sniffed and cleared his throat. "Going to bed. We had... we'd just decided where to take our vacation this summer." His breath shuddered out, "I was gonna propose on the beach." Tears streamed down his face as his lower lip quivered. I could practically feel his heart breaking.

"Do you remember seeing anyone in your house, any odd noises or smells?"

He shook his head. "No, we said good night, and we went to sleep. Until that thing woke me. It told me to...to kill her," his voice hitched. "I don't understand why I did it, I love her. I would never hurt her!"

"Fae compulsion is hard to overcome, especially if you're not expecting it," I explained to him. I leaned down behind Richard's head. "If it hasn't been that long, can we go by the crime scene? I can do that spell I did at Howard's, get a glimpse of the fae."

He nodded and turned back to the suspect. "Okay. We'll be back later. Are you hungry or thirsty? We can get you something?"

He nodded and wiped his cheeks. "I am a little hungry."

"Okay, I'll get Officer Hyde to bring you something. You just sit tight." He nodded. His shaky breathing seemed to echo in the small room. Richard got to his feet, and we got the address from Hyde and drove straight there.

———

The scene was a few blocks from Richard's house. There was still crime scene tape across the front door and one squad car parked in the driveway. Other than that, the scene was clear. Richard parked on the street, and I walked straight into the house, ducking under the yellow tape. I could hear Richard arguing with someone outside, probably a newbie who was wondering who the hell I was and what did I think I was doing. It wasn't the first time that happened, and it wouldn't be the last.

I placed my palms together, letting my magic fill the room. I pointed my right hand down, keeping my palms together.

"Spirits, show me the crime that happened here. Show me how Jordan lost his love." I walked towards the bedroom where she was killed as the ghostly image of Jordan on the bed, strangling his girlfriend appeared. I looked around the room, and in the corner, there was indeed someone there. The light surrounding it was too bright, but I could tell it wasn't a fae. It was tall, taller than Richard, and wide. I knew fae came in all shapes and sizes, but this didn't make sense. I still had my onyx stone in my pocket, and it was vibrating just a little, which was odd. I'd expect it to be dancing in my hand this close to the suspect.

I turned back to the scene on the bed, and Richard walked in. "See anything."

"Yeah." Jordan got to his knees and stared at the creature in the corner. A tear rolled down his cheek. As if killing his girlfriend was the complete opposite of what he would do, and his heart knew that. The creature pointed at him, and he nodded and picked up his cell phone. I assume this is when he called 911. I turned back to the creature, and it seemed to calmly walk from the room, so I followed. "Something did tell him to do it. But I'm not sure what it was. Not fae, but something else that can enthrall. There's a little fae magic, but a lot less than I expected." The glowing creature faded to nothing in the living room as the spell ended. I stood in the living room and closed my eyes.

"Are you all right?" Richard walked up behind me and put his hands on my shoulders.

"You know, I've seen some dreadful things. I've seen friends dead and creatures torn limb from limb, but there's something about watching it happen that just," I hugged myself. "I know that spell is helpful, but I don't like it."

He stepped closer, and I heard him whisper. "I'm sorry, sweetheart." I felt him kiss the back of my head.

"It's gonna take a bit to get that out of my head."

He rubbed my arms and gave them a little squeeze. "Whatever I can do to help."

I heard loud footsteps walking in the house. "You two done making out? Can I close up the crime scene now?"

"Hey!" Richard yelled at whoever it was. I don't think I ever heard him mad before. "Show some damn respect, rookie. Roa is more dedicated than half the precinct. Her job is hard, and she doesn't need your attitude."

"It's okay, Moss," I turned to the door, and like I expected, I didn't know that officer. He was new. "He didn't know. You can close it up." I walked past him towards Richard's car, and it was clear his tone of voice got to the newbie officer.

"I'm sorry, Ma'am." He actually sounded sorry.

I shook my head but didn't turn. "It's okay, you didn't know." I heard Richard say something else to the officer before following me out. I leaned against the car and felt it unlock, so I let myself in, and Richard quickly slid into the driver's seat.

"I'm sorry," he said and held my hand.

I turned to him, his words took me off guard. "For what?"

"I didn't mean to lose my temper like that. I knew you were having a tough time, and he clearly didn't care. It pissed me off."

I patted his hand. "It's okay, I get it. Hopefully, he'll spread the word to be respectful. But I'm used to it. I don't take it personally."

"I know," he reached over and laid his hand on my neck and rubbed my muscles. "But I'm not, and the fact that you are just says how much they never appreciated you. I hope we can change that." I looked over at him, and he leaned over and gave me a little kiss. It was a risk, but I trusted his window tints and the fact the rookie wouldn't dare look at us. So, I didn't push him away and enjoyed the feel of his lips on mine.

"That would be nice. But I'm so used to it that it's going to take a lot on both sides, I bet."

He nodded. "I'll help however I can." From the way he looked at me, I believed him.

———

An hour later, we were still at our desks working on the paperwork. My email was finally set up, so I filled out the parts of the report that I dealt with. I lowered the keyboard a bit, and thankfully seemed to help with my wrist. I didn't want to pour ibuprofen down my throat all day just to do my job. My arms broke out in goosebumps, and I saw Will sit in the chair next to my desk.

"Feelin' better, Hen?" I shrugged. "Bad un?" I nodded. He pursed his lips out, and I held back a chuckle. "Sorry, Hen."

That was the second time he called me 'Hen.' "Why are you calling me that? You hardly ever called me that before."

He wiggled his eyebrows. "You don't like it?"

I snickered. "I didn't say that."

"You like it, you like it," he sing-songed as he walked around me before sitting on my desk. I did my best to hide my smile as I shook my head. Of course, I liked it. I just wasn't sure why he was calling me that all of a sudden. "When I saw your scar, Hen, it scared me. You were hurt, bad, and I dinnae know where ya were. I figured it'd help me feel better, too, if I could say something nice."

I typed a few letters before I looked over at him. "Okay. I guess you can keep calling me that." He snickered. "How'd you make my arm feel better?"

He swung his legs back and forth. "Ya cannae tell?"

"No, why would I know that?" I turned back to my computer and continued typing. "You barely touch me."

"That's cause ya see me comin'." He reached out and laid his fingers on my right hand. I felt his cold fingers on my skin. "Cold helps pain all the time."

"Makes sense." I looked up at him. "Thank you." He gave me a wink, and I watched him walk over to Hyde's desk and smell the bowl of butterscotch on it before walking away, his hands linked behind his back. I did my best not to look at the horrid wound on the back of his head. Hopefully, he didn't suffer because it looked painful. I turned to Richard, who had just hung up his phone. "Lunch?" We scarfed breakfast since we had a suspect to question, so I was looking forward to something substantial in my stomach and soon.

"Sure. Want to invite Nicola?" I nodded and gave her a quick text. "So, how did he help your arm?"

I smiled at how attentive he was. "You heard that?"

"I always notice when you talk to Will." The way he said it, he wasn't jealous, just observant.

I rubbed my arm, glad something could help the annoying pain. "Said cold helps pain."

He nodded, giving it a thought. "Makes sense. You could mention it to your physical therapist next week. They might have some exercises to keep the pain from being so much."

"Maybe." I heard the familiar clacking of Nicola's expensive heels coming up the stairs, and I turned. She was wearing a white shirt and a bright yellow knee-length skirt.

"I don't know about you, but I need some meat in my mouth."

I laughed and got to my feet. "Burgers?"

"God, yes." We all piled into Richard's car, and he drove us to Sal's. It was the lunch rush, which in this town was like eight people. The waitress, Larisa, smiled when she saw us walk in.

"Hey! Table for three?"

"That'd be great, thanks." She gathered up some menus, and we followed her back to a booth. Richard slid in, and I slid in after while Nicola sat across from us. "I'll be right back with some water, and Lily?" I looked up at her. "Thank you for your help."

I smiled at her. "Anytime, Larisa, it's no trouble." She walked away, and Nicola leaned forward.

"What did you do?"

"Performed a cord cutting for her. Her ex wouldn't leave her alone, and she wanted to move on."

Nicola sat back and nodded. "Glad it worked, nothing worse than an ex who won't take a hint."

"I know, right?" Honestly, I didn't know. All my exes tended to run for the hills when the relationship was over. Anything to separate themselves from the weirdo. Larisa sat down three glasses of ice water and me, and Nicola ordered cheeseburgers, and Richard got a turkey club. "So, before our food gets there," I leaned closer to Nicola. No one around us needed to hear us talking about murder. "You didn't see anything odd about our newest domestic violence victim, did you?"

Nicola sighed. "No, she was strangled, and from the measurements I had Hyde get, they matched the suspect's hands. No drugs in their systems either." I leaned forward and stared at the sugar packets on the table.

Richard put a hand on my back. "Whatcha thinking?"

"That this is going to be harder to figure out than I originally thought."

"You mean because of that shape in the room?"

Nicola shifted. "What shape?" I sat back and turned to both of them and told Nicola about what I saw in the house. "And you aren't convinced it was fae? I mean, I'm no expert, but they come in all kinds of sizes, right?"

I nodded. "They do, but I haven't heard of any *that* big. Tall and lanky for sure, short, and squat absolutely, human-sized, yes, but not taller and wider than Richard." Richard blew out a low whistle at that. "But there was fae magic. My stone didn't lie. I expected it to buzz so much it'd start a fire in my pocket." Nicola chuckled and took a sip of her water. "Instead, it sort of gently buzzed like the magic was far away."

They both leaned on the table, their heads in their hands. "I think I need to study more on preternatural things," Richard said.

I reached over and rubbed his arm. "I can help with that."

Nicola laughed. "Like that study session wouldn't end in sex." I laughed, and Richard shook his head with a smile as Larisa brought our food. It was just in time, too. My stomach had started growling. Our cheeseburgers were juicy and perfect with fresh tomatoes and mayo, and the fries were crispy. Richard was enjoying his club as well. They used apple-smoked bacon, and it went well with the juicy turkey slices. Never trust anyone who turns their nose up at greasy spoons.

———

When we got back to the precinct, Hyde brought over the victim's cell phone. "There was no forensic evidence on it," he said, "so we can look through it before it's given to a lawyer."

It was in a big plastic bag, and I took it from him. "Thanks, Hyde." He nodded with a close-lipped smile and sat at his own desk. I opened the bag and took the phone out. I laid it on my desk and put my hands on either side of it and closed my eyes. I wanted to know what she felt the last time she held that phone. I had to know if there was truly love in that home before such an evil act took place. I snapped my fingers, and the little tea candle on my desk lit up. I had been using a lot of raw magic lately, and I needed to get back in the habit of using a medium to help me. I had a few little candles on my desk for that. I figured they were small enough that no one would bitch about them. I needed to put some other things on my desk at work as well so I wouldn't have to keep running home for things.

"Don't start a fire now, Roa." I heard an officer behind me tease. I lifted my middle finger without looking, and the bullpen erupted in laughter. I kept my smile in check as I took a deep breath and picked up the phone. My magic flew around it, looking for remnants of emotions. It didn't take long. I gasped as love flowed into me. It was strong and unwavering. She loved him with her whole self, as did he. Glass would never have willingly killed her.

My arms broke out in goosebumps before I heard him. "Whatcha doing there, my bonny Hen?" I opened my eyes, and they were teary. I didn't expect that. Will's playful smile disappeared as he leaned closer to my face. "What's wrong?"

I took in a shaky breath. "He wouldn't have killed her. He

loved her, she loved him."

He looked concerned for a moment. "You feel their fear?" He looked between me and the phone a few times. "Maybe you shouldn't touch it."

"No, not their fear, their love." I reached up with my free hand and laid it on his cheek. I wanted him to feel what I did. Someone else had to know of their love. If a ghost needed to breathe, he would have gasped. His eyes went wide as he stared at me, his hand landing on mine.

"What?" His voice was barely a whisper.

"What was that?" I heard Richard's chair squeak, and I assumed he turned to me. But I kept my eyes on Will.

"Oh, my bonny Hen, I knew it." He moved his hand, and I lowered mine.

"Knew what?" Will just smiled and touched my cheek before he disappeared.

"Lily, you all right?" I turned to Richard, and he looked worried.

"Yeah," I wiped my eyes. "I wanted to make sure they loved each other. They did. He didn't willingly do this."

He scooted his chair closer and touched my knee. "And we'll do whatever we can to prove that."

———

That night, I was sitting on my couch while Richard prattled around my kitchen, making dinner. He was good at turning random bits of things into meals. I had some show playing on the TV, but I wasn't paying attention to it. The memory of that poor girl being strangled by the man she loved kept playing over and over in my mind. Knowing how much she loved him, I could practically feel her heartbreak as she stared at him, unable to stop him. The betrayal she must have felt, having the man she loved, who wanted to marry her, kill her. I sniffed and wiped my eyes.

"Sweetheart?"

Richard's voice woke me from the horrible vision. "Hmm?" I turned, and he had two plates in his hands.

"Dinner's ready." I managed a smile as he walked over to the couch and set the plates on the table.

"Thanks." He made mashed potatoes, baked chicken, and honey carrots. "You spoil me."

"You deserve it." He kissed my forehead, and I picked up my fork and put it in the potatoes but didn't eat. "Still can't get her out of your head?"

"No." I finally took a bite of the potatoes. He had made them for me before, so I knew they were going to be good. They were fluffy and buttery, the perfect side carb.

"Is there anything I can do to help?" I watched him cut into his chicken and take a bite. He was a big proponent of taking care of yourself so you can take care of others. I loved that about him.

I nodded. "Yeah, after dinner." He gave me a wink, and I looked back at my dinner and steeled myself to eat it. "So, who taught you how to cook anyway?"

He swallowed a bite of carrot. "My mom. She taught all three of us. She said you have to know how to cook so you can take care of someone. You can't properly care for them if you can't cook them a simple meal."

I chuckled. "I get that. Well, she did an excellent job, and you were a good student."

He gave me a wink. "I had a lot of practice in college. When me and some friends moved into a house off campus, I was the only one who could cook."

"Ugh, helpless men are such a turn-off."

He laughed and wrapped his arm around me. "Spoken like a woman who knew too many."

"Unfortunately, yes." I leaned into him. "But not anymore."

———

After dinner, I pulled him to the bedroom and turned on my sound system. I picked a playlist that was full of soft, soothing flutes and thick stringed chords, and I turned the lights down. "When I have a bad day, and I can't get it out of my mind, I meditate." I took his hand and pulled him to the bed. "Will you try it with me?"

He put a hand on my cheek. "Of course, anything to help."

I gave him a little kiss. "Get comfy." I changed into a light pink silk nightgown, and he stripped to his boxer briefs.

He walked over to me, and his hands wrapped around my waist. "Don't you look gorgeous?" He smiled as his hands ran up the cool fabric. "I don't think I've seen you in this one."

"I don't think you've seen me in anything but giant t-shirts." I chuckled and hugged him before I pulled him over to the bed. "Lay down."

"Yes, ma'am." I watched him crawl onto the bed and lay down on his back. I followed suit, laying on my back above the covers. I reached out, and he held my hand. "Have you ever meditated before?"

"No, I never thought my mind had the patience for it."

The corner of my mouth tilted up. "You might have been doing the wrong kind for you. My mind was always too busy for just music. I needed something to guide me, to tell me where to go and focus my mind on that instead of the horrors of the day."

"Did you meditate after Howard was killed?"

I turned to look at him and met his eyes. "No, I mourned him the old-fashioned way. With drinks and stories." He gave a little chuckle. "Tonight, my mind needs to be quiet." I gave his hand a squeeze and closed my eyes as I faced the ceiling. "Close your eyes and think about a little cottage in the woods. It's happy and safe. What does your house look like?"

"Small, grass roof, flowers around it."

"Mine has windows on either side of the door, there's a flower box under each, and there's different colored pansies in each box. The door is dark blue, and it's surrounded by wildflowers. Behind the house, there's a path. My path is dirt and made from how many times I've made this trek, and it goes into the woods."

I squeezed his hand, letting him know it was his turn. "My path is stone but well-worn from travel and goes into a field with tall grass."

"As I walk into the woods, I soon come to a door. It's big, made of wood, and circular. There are old brass fittings on it, and when I push it open, it makes a deep groaning noise."

I squeezed his hand. "My door is white and looks like the door to my childhood home, and when I open it, I can smell fresh baked cookies."

That made me smile. "Behind the door is a room made of marble. In this room, we see whatever we want to see. There are no windows, the room opens up to the skies, and there's a big comfy couch, and I lay down on it. Above me, the stars glitter, and I can see colorful galaxies swirling in space."

"That sounds lovely." I felt his hand tighten on mine, and in my mind, I saw him walking towards me. "I see a beach under the stars, and sitting on a big couch is the most beautiful woman I've ever seen." I smiled but didn't open my eyes. "She smiles when she sees me walking towards her."

"I see a handsome man in loose cotton pants, no shirt for

some reason," he chuckled. "He's walking over and sits next to me, and what's this? He picks up my feet and starts rubbing them." Richard's laughter rang through the apartment, and I squeezed his hand.

"I rub her feet until they feel brand new, then I slowly crawl up her body, kissing as I go." I saw him in my mind's eyes, doing this, and I gasped when I thought I actually felt his kisses on my body. I watched as his hands snaked up my torso and cupped my breast. I couldn't stop the little gasp when I felt that pressure in real life. But I know it wasn't him. His hand was still in mine, and the bed hadn't moved.

"I reach up and hold his face as it hovers over mine," I heard Richard gasp. "And I bring his lips to mine." In my mind's eye, we kissed, and his arms slid around me. "I can feel how much he wants me," my voice was sultry, and the corner of my mouth tilted in a smile. "And I want to show him how much I want him." I pulled him down on top of me, and I felt the soft couch under my back and a wonderful pressure as he laid on top of me.

"Oh, Lily, why do I feel you?" He moaned as his hand tightened around mine.

"I don't know, but I like it." In my mind's eye, he kissed down my neck, and I felt his lips even though he was still next to me.

"Me too." I watched as his fingers slid under the thin straps of my nightgown and slide them down my arms. He kissed my bare shoulder, and I shivered as my hand ran up his neck and buried it in his hair. It was soft like it always was, and I had no idea what was going on, but it was clear we both liked it. The way he was taking his time, I felt my nipples harden at the feel of my nightgown being pulled over them. I watched as his eyes took in my body, my hips, my stomach, my breasts.

"God, Lily, you're so fucking beautiful."

I laughed as his hand ran up my stomach and cupped my breast. "You think so?" I reached down and cupped his hard dick. He moaned and closed his eyes as I gently squeezed him.

"I know so."

————

When we woke, it seemed like we had fallen asleep while meditating. We were still above the covers, holding hands. Which was definitely not how we fell asleep in the dream. Him on top of me, our legs tangled, and my arms around him. The things we did in that dream were things that I'd never had happen while meditating. I wasn't sure how it happened, but I had a feeling he wouldn't mind doing some science experiments on it. I smiled at the memory of what we did, and I turned to him. His eyes were still closed, and he was breathing deep with sleep. There was a little smile on his face, like he dreamed the same thing I did.

Richard breathed in deep and turned towards me. "Man, it's been a while since I slept that deep."

I smiled. "Me too."

He rolled over and kissed my cheek. "Did that actually happen?"

"I think in some way it did, but I can't wait to do that physically."

He chuckled. "Me either. How do you feel?"

I reached over and laid a hand on his cheek. "Better. Thanks for doing that with me."

"You got it. You were right, I need that prompt, or my mind can't focus."

"That's my favorite way to meditate. What do you say we stop by a coffee shop for a treat before work? I don't think I've taken you to my favorite spot."

He smiled. "You don't like coffee but have a favorite coffee shop?"

My alarm went off, and I quickly touched the button to quiet it. "I do."

———

We stood in line at Jolly Bear Baristas, and I was happy to introduce Richard to it. A girl had to be careful when introducing your significant others to your favorite spots. Nothing worse than running into an ex while at a place you thought was a haven. But there was something about Richard that told me it was okay to show him this. Mabon moved to town a few years ago and opened his own coffee shop. He had the usual drinks and goodies you'd find. Along with a few new things that everyone looked forward to when it was time. Everything he made was a hit. Star-who? It was our turn to order, and Mabon was working the register. He was a big guy, more muscular than Richard and a few inches taller, but that was to be expected. He was a bear shifter. His auburn beard was neatly trimmed, and his hair was in a long ponytail behind his head.

"How are you today, Miss Lily?" He asked with a big smile, his deep voice almost booming around the room.

"I'm good, Mabon, and yourself?"

"Can't complain. Is this the famous Richard I've heard so much about?" He held out his hand, and Richard gave it a shake.

"It is, Richard Moss, nice to meet you."

"Mabon Bell, a pleasure. So," he clapped his hands together. "What can I get you? Lily, are you ready to try my coffee yet?" I saw a hopeful smile on his face, but he knew I hated coffee.

I grimaced. "No. My usual, please."

He chuckled as he grabbed a cup and wrote on it. "How

about you, sir?"

"Black for me, medium." I pressed my card on the reader, and it gave a happy beep that said I was six dollars poorer.

Mabon grabbed another cup and wrote Richard's order on it. "Easy enough, they'll be right out. It was nice to meet you."

"Nice to meet you as well."

Mabon leaned down towards me. "Tell Nicola I said hi?"

I smiled and gave him a wink. "You got it." We went and stood by the end of the counter and waited for our drinks. I really liked this place. It was mostly full of new people in town, so it was rare when I'd get a sneer from someone in here. And if Mabon saw anyone acting that way towards his customers, he'd put a stop to it immediately. I appreciated that about him.

Richard leaned down to my ear. "That dude is big." He sounded impressed, and I giggled.

"He's a shifter. Can you guess what kind?"

I watched Richard study the big man for a moment. "Wolf would be too obvious," I nodded. "Shark." I couldn't stop the laugh that came out of me with that guess. Richard wrapped his arms around me and kissed my head.

"I don't think were-sharks are a thing."

He kept his arms around me and gave me a kiss. "Bear."

I stood on my toes and gave his cheek a kiss. "Good job!"

"So," his lips lingered on my cheek. "You told him about me?"

"Of course I did. I had to talk to someone about you besides Nicola."

"Lily and Her hunky man?" The young girl who read the names on the cups sounded confused, but she put them down anyway. I laughed and picked them up and handed Richard his.

"Bye, Mabon!" He gave me a wink, and we walked outside.

"Isn't he fun," Richard snickered and took a drink. "Mm, good coffee, though."

"His drinks are always good. I've been trying to set him and Nicola up for ages."

"Shifters not her type?" We slid into his car, and he started for the precinct.

"She's only ever dated humans, but maybe if we both suggest it, she'll go for it?"

He laughed. "Maybe. So, there are some people in town you get along with?"

"Oh yeah, not many, though. They're all new folks like Mabon and Nicola, but I'm so used to keeping to myself I don't really reach out much. I'm thinking that was a mistake." Over the last six months, while I had been at my most vulnerable, I had also been the least alone I'd ever been since my cousin left town. I didn't realize I was so lonely, and I felt like I was ready to start making more friends.

He took another drink of his coffee. "You ever date a shifter?"

"No," I took a drink of my iced chai. The amount of cinnamon and brown sugar was absolutely perfect. "None of them seemed interested, so I stuck with humans."

"The shifters aren't rude like humans, are they?"

I gave my drink a little shake. "No, not that I've experienced. I mean, I've gotten a few off of some trumped-up or fake charges over the years, so I'm friendly with the community, as small as it is. But none of them ever asked me out."

He chuckled and gave my thigh a little squeeze. "You could have asked them out."

I turned to him, trying to hide my smile. "I am aware I could have asked, but I am a chicken shit when it comes to those things." He laughed, and the sound made my smile appear. "Remember, you were the one who kissed me first."

He gasped like he was flabbergasted. "You weren't going to kiss me?"

I don't ever remember being with someone who made me laugh so much. "Admittedly, I had wanted to kiss you for a while at that point. But I was more worried about keeping you alive so I could kiss you later." I poked him in the chest.

He nodded and took a drink of his coffee. "I get that. Hard to date if you're dead."

"True." I looked down at my hands for a moment. "Do you think Ryan might tell us we can't date *and* work together?"

I watched him think it over. "Fraternization is frowned upon, but you aren't a cop, and that rule is mainly for the officers. You're official now, but still not a cop. I think if we can stay professional at work, we shouldn't have a problem." He sounded so optimistic. I hoped it rubbed off on me.

"I hope not." I patted that hand that lingered on my thigh. "I don't want to lose you. You're the best thing that's happened to me in a long time."

He gave me a little smile. "You're the best thing to happen to me too, Sweetheart."

———

When we got to our desks, I saw familiar purple hair in Ryan's office, and I gasped. "Gwendalyn is here!"

"Who's Gwendalyn?" Richard hung his jacket on his coat rack and sat down.

I turned to him, my hands on my hips. "The other witch!"

"Oh right," he looked in the direction of Ryan's office. "Hope she works out."

"Me too." I watched as Hyde walked over, and he had a

book in his hands. "Morning, Hyde." He took the chair next to my desk and put the book on it. "You know, I don't think I know your first name." I looked at his name tag, but it just had R. Hyde on it.

He cleared his throat. "It's Remy."

I smiled. "Remy Hyde, that's quite a name."

"Isn't it?" He seemed a little embarrassed. It's probably why he went by his last name so often.

"Whatcha got?" I motioned to the book.

"Well, I got curious about our ghost friend and was able to find him in one of the books about the founding of the town in the library."

My eyes went wide. "Really?" He smiled and opened to a page he had bookmarked, and there on the page was Will. Alive and smiling with other people, maybe his family. He looked so happy. I trailed my fingers along his face, he looked the same, but there was just something more alive in his eyes. My arms broke out in goosebumps, and I saw him lean over my shoulder from the corner of my eye.

"Well, isn't that a handsome lookin' fella'" he teased.

I chuckled. "You look the same." My eyes moved to the caption on the photo. Pictured the McKay family, Ruben, William, Niall, Callen, 1845, taken a week before William was murdered by his brother Ruben. I gasped and tried to cover the text, but my entire body broke out in goosebumps. He had seen it. I turned to Will, his eyes were wide, and his jaw was slack.

"Ru?"

"Will," I reached up and put my hand on his cheek. He was cold, and my hand was tingling with magic. "Look at me, look at me, please." But his eyes didn't move from that picture.

"Roa, what's wrong?" Hyde looked between me and

Richard, who finally turned.

"Lily, what is it?" But I kept my attention on Will.

He let out a sob as ghostly tears ran from his eyes. "My own brother? How could he? I loved him. We were family!" His voice broke my heart.

"I don't know, Will, but it's all right. It was a long time ago." Another sob escaped his lips. "Will, please look at me." He finally turned to me, his lower lip trembling as his ghostly tears ran down my hand, leaving cold trails down my arm. "Whatever happened was a long time ago. You've been here with us for years. The past is the past—"

"But it's my past, Hen." I had never heard him so upset before. It was heartbreaking. "How did I not know my own brother killed me?"

"Trauma, it keeps most ghosts from knowing what happened because it hurts." At least, that's what everyone theorized. We didn't really know why. It probably had something to do with the fact that ghosts were just energy, not any bit of a soul from a departed person.

His lips frowned so hard I had never seen him so sad. "It does hurt, Hen, it does." He went invisible, and I knew he moved away from me.

"Will, don't, whatever it is, don't please!" I stood, and a few of the officers turned to me a moment before the air was filled with loose paper. People stood and shouted as he moved, invisible from desk to desk, throwing whatever he could in the air and on the ground. Plants were toppled over and chairs thrown. "Will stop, please!" But there was nothing I could do or say that would stop him. He was too upset.

Richard stood next to me and watched. "What happened?"

"He found out his brother killed him."

He grimaced. "Shit."

Hyde stood next to me. "I'm sorry I didn't think he'd get upset. I just thought it would be nice if he saw his brothers." He genuinely looked like he was sorry as he watched the bullpen turn into a tornado of papers and trash.

I nodded. "It's not your fault, Hyde." My eyes slid to Ryan's office. He and Gwendalyn were standing in the doorway, watching the scene. The witch's eyes were wide, her mouth making a little 'o'. Ryan was shaking his head. He looked disappointed and motioned for Gwendalyn to follow him back to his office.

"Shit." I heard Richard mumble next to me. Shit indeed.

———

I tried for an hour to get Will to stop, but no matter how hard I tried, I just couldn't reach him. He was too upset. I could barely eat dinner that night. I couldn't stop wondering how long he was going to be like that. Because it did occur to me that Ryan might finally do something drastic about him.

———

The next morning, I felt better. The bad stuff from the last few days was slowly moving to the back of my mind. I was still annoyed that Richard and I didn't have the time we wanted for each other, but we'd get there. And I was still worried about Will, but I hadn't seen him when we walked into the bullpen, and I figured he was still sulking somewhere. So, I'd let him do that until he felt better and started bugging me again. Which I hoped was soon.

I sat at my desk, and Richard's chair squeaked as he sat down. I sat still and concentrated for a moment but couldn't sense Will. I hoped he had calmed down by now.

"Ms. Roa?" I looked up and saw Gwendalyn next to my

desk. "I'm Gwen, the new witch." She held out her hand, and I smiled.

I stood and took her hand. "Nice to meet you. You can call me Lily," I shook her hand. She had a good, firm handshake.

"Lily, nice to meet you. I can't tell you how excited I am to be here." She clasped her hands under her chin, and I couldn't help but chuckle at her enthusiasm.

"I'm glad to have more help. I was hoping at some point you'd let me see your conjuring space, that way, I can see if you need anything, or I could learn something. I can show you mine as well." I remember doing this when Jackson and Amelia moved to town. I will never forget how fucking impressed I was at their witchy room. I learned a lot about organization that day.

"That sounds great! I'm not doing anything at the moment. We could go now?"

I smiled, "Yeah—" then I remembered. "Oh, I don't have my car." Richard and I had gotten into the habit of using his. I haven't even driven since I got my sling off.

She waved her hand. "That's okay. I got mine."

"Perfect!" I turned to Richard. "Us witches will be back later. We have official witchy stuff to do. If you need me, call."

"Will do." He gave me that gorgeous smile, and we walked down to the morgue to get to the parking garage. I didn't see Nicola on the way out. Maybe she had a late night. I followed Gwen to her car, a little blue bug, and I told her how to get to my apartment. It was closest, so we figured we'd start there. She had a strawberry air freshener hanging off her rear-view mirror, and it must have been new because it was so strong I knew when I got out of her car, the smell would linger on me.

"So, how'd you end up moving across the country for this job?"

She kept her eyes on the road as she talked. "I needed a change, and Arion seemed like a nice town."

I nodded. "It is. It has its challenges, like all towns, but I love it. Where are you staying?"

"On Rose St, renting a little house. I swear it makes me feel like an actual adult, renting a house instead of an apartment."

I chuckled. "I can see that."

She pulled up to my building and nodded in approval. "Nice looking building."

"It's great. Everyone's quiet, and no one burns my mail." Her eyes went wide. "That was a joke." Thankfully, all the other tenants were newcomers, or I might actually worry about my mail.

She sighed in relief and smiled. "Oh, good." We walked up to my apartment, and I unlocked the door. The morning sun was streaming in the windows, and it still smelled like the baked chicken Richard made the night before. "Wow."

"Nice, right? I love it." She stepped inside my witchy room and looked around. Like a good witch, she didn't touch anything, but her eyes took in everything I had. When she looked down and saw the boxes scattered around, she pointed at them. "No room?"

"Not yet. Those books were given to me after my friends died. They were the only other witches in town. Did Ryan tell you about them?"

She nodded, more subdued. "The Fells, right? So sad."

"Have you ever worked with police before?" I watched her walk around the repurposed morgue table in the middle of my witchy room.

"A few times, but they always brought me to the morgue. I was never at a crime scene at the same time as a victim."

I nodded. "Well, that'll change here. You'll go to crime scenes, and you'll see some gnarly stuff. Are you ready for that?"

She sniffed at my herbs. "I always thought that would be one of those situations where you wouldn't know how you'd act until it happened." She stood straight and turned to me. "But I've seen some gnarly things spiritually, too, so I think I'll be okay."

"Good." I gave her a smile, "But I'm here, and there's a counselor at the precinct twenty-four-seven if anyone needs it, including us."

"Gotcha. I like how you keep your herbs, it's colorful." I kept them in rainbow order, ones good for spells that hurt someone were in red pots, and herbs good for healing were in blue. Of course, there was a lot more green than other colors, but you could still tell.

"Thanks, I think it spruces up the place. Do you have any questions?"

She chuckled. "About a million, but I'll narrow it down to at least a thousand. Are you on call all day and night?"

"Depends, I think since there's two of us now, we can work out how we want to do that. If we want to do it weekly, bi-weekly, or monthly. We'll tell them what we'd like, and we'll start there. Any preference?"

"Hmm, how about monthly? I think it'd be nice to have a whole month not on call."

"Same, that sounds good. Do you know who you'll work with yet?"

She shook her head. "No, not yet. Any suggestions?" I crossed my arms and reached up to the little rainbow suncatcher and gave it a tap. Colors danced around us when the perfect suggestion came to mind.

"Well, Hyde has been coming around a lot lately. He

might work out well? He's not a detective, but I think that's been a coincidence with me. I don't see why you couldn't work with anyone."

She nodded and looked at the picture of my family I had in the room. "Hyde, all right, I'll ask. What's something they always ask you to do?"

I chuckled. "Do you know the Praeteria Spell?

Gwen laughed and nodded. "Oh yeah."

"Not that I end up doing it every time. Most of the time, I get there too late for that spell." She looked up at the wall and saw the little drawing that Richard did of the elements. After I got released from the hospital, I asked him if I could have it. He brought it the next day, framed and everything.

"Interesting drawing." Her head cocked to the side. "Is that a boob?"

I laughed and walked over. "My partner drew it. It was part of our last big case. I'll tell you about it sometime."

She turned to me, her hands clasped behind her. "I think you've given me a lot of promising ideas. Shall we go to my witchy room?"

I smiled. "We shall." I had a feeling Gwen was going to work out great. We chatted while she drove over to her little house that was three blocks away from Richard's. I learned she loved horror movies and was allergic to dogs, and she was the first person in her family to move out of their hometown. When she pulled into her driveway, I saw her front lawn was filled with all kinds of flowers and herbs. Clearly, they were planted magically, as nothing would grow that fast.

"I love your lawn," I leaned down and smelled one of the tulips. "Richard said—" I stopped but then realized it was just a lawn, so I pretended to clear my throat. "Richard said I could plant whatever I wanted in his yard since I live in an apartment. I honestly can't wait to start."

"That's nice of him," she unlocked the door, and we stepped inside. "How come you haven't started?" Inside looked like the typical 'just moved from out of state' look, a single recliner in front of a TV, boxes full of pictures around the room. Her dining room only had bookshelves at the moment with half the shelves full.

"Waiting for the all clear from a physical therapist on my shoulder." I showed her the scar, and her eyes went wide.

"Right, the Major said you lost your entire arm last year. That must have been scary."

"Everything before that was scary," I admitted. "I hardly registered this when it happened." I sniffed the air. It smelled like snickerdoodle cookies. "You got a candle or something?"

"Wax melts," she pointed to a wax melter on top of a short bookcase. It was a black cat wearing a pointed witches hat standing before a cauldron. "Doesn't it smell good?"

"Making me hungry." We laughed, and I followed her to the second bedroom, where she put her conjuring space. Like I expected, it was completely put together, unlike the rest of the house. It was immaculate, and a sense of peace fell over me as we walked in. "What a lovely space, Gwen. You've done really well." One wall was nothing but bookshelves that were filled with books. The wall where the window was had her herbs. Some were in swinging baskets that hung from the ceiling. The other wall was covered in little shelves that had crystals and charms from all over the world.

"Thanks. I really like it.

"It's peaceful and organized, a perfect place to do magic." A rolling meow made my ear twitch, and I turned to the doorway.

A white cat with two different colored eyes was rubbing on the doorframe. "Aww, kitty." I kneeled down, and the cat pranced over and rubbed on my outstretched hands.

"I was surprised you didn't have a cat at your apartment." She leaned against a tall table, crossing her arms.

"Not allowed, no garden, no cat, it's like I'm half a witch." I teased, and Gwen snickered. "But it's affordable, and I really do like it. One day, perhaps. What's their name?"

'My name is Malin.' I heard in my head and gasped as the cat, Malin, kept rubbing on my fingers.

"You have a legit familiar?" I looked up at Gwen, my eyes wide. It had been a long time since I met a familiar. Last time, I was around ten, I think, and I remember being so sad when my cousin pulled me away from the pretty black cat before I could learn its name. I never saw it again.

"I do, got her when I was thirteen." I never had a familiar, my cousin wouldn't let animals into the apartment, and of course, where I live, now I couldn't have any either. I wonder if Richard was allergic to anything.

"It's nice to meet you, Malin."

'And you. You've done well with your arm.' She gave me one more rub and walked from the room.

I stood up. "She's so pretty."

Gwen chuckled. "And she knows it too." I walked over to her bookcases and perused the titles. "I'm sure I'm missing something I need. Are there any good stores in town?"

"Hm, you have to go over to Woodhurst. There aren't any witchy stores in town."

She turned, and I could see she was shocked at that. "Oh, weird."

I turned, crossing my arms over my stomach. "So, while

the job is good, the town is...not as friendly towards some magical types. You might see people turn their noses up at me or just plain yell at me to leave. So that might happen to you when it gets out that you're a witch as well. The Fells were really good at ignoring it, but they had each other to lean on."

She bit her lower lip and leaned against her bookcase. "I wondered about that." She stood straight, and I could see how determined she was not to let the haters get to her. "But I'll be okay."

"If it gets too much, let me know. I'll see if there's something I can do."

"Thanks."

"Well," I clapped my hands together, "why don't we go back to the precinct? I'll introduce you to Hyde."

She smiled and gave a nod. "Sounds good."

———

We were about five blocks from the precinct when I felt my phone buzz. I took it out of my pocket and saw Nicola had texted: *You need to get back to the station. Ryan told that new witch to get rid of Will!*

My eyes went wide. "Ryan told you to get rid of Will?" I turned to her as she drove, and she glanced at me for a moment.

"Oh yeah, yesterday after he made a mess of the bullpen. Why, were you gonna do it?"

My jaw dropped when I heard her say that. "No, I wasn't going to do it!" She looked shocked at the sudden volume of my voice, and I don't blame her. I'd barely known her for three hours, and I was yelling. "He was upset. He just found out how he died. He just needed time!"

She stumbled over her words for a moment. "I, just, sorry he told me to. I did it all the time back east."

I sighed and shook my head. "I'm sorry. I didn't mean to yell. I was just shocked." I laid my hand on her arm, hoping it would enforce that I wasn't mad at her. Last thing I wanted to do was get off on the wrong foot with her. "Ryan has been after me to exorcize him for years, but I refuse to do it. He's not really a menace. He just has more energy than most ghosts. He said he'd calm down for me, but yesterday, he learned that his brother killed him. It really upset him. I'll talk with him when we get back. I'll get him to apologize." I noticed she kept glancing at me. "What?"

"I...I already did it." Her voice was quiet, and I felt my heart stop.

"What?"

The poor girl looked like she was about to cry. "He asked me to do it last night, so I did. I didn't realize I shouldn't have, I'm so sorry."

I felt my beating heart pounding in my chest. "No."

"I'm sorry, I'm so sorry." Her voice was thick with emotion, and I really hoped I didn't make her cry.

I did my best to keep my own tears in, and I laid my hand on her arm again. "Where is he? Did he cross over?" The thought of never seeing Will again was breaking my heart. I didn't even get to say goodbye.

"I don't know, I don't think so. I didn't feel him leave like that. He was just forced out of the building." I felt a little better knowing he wasn't gone for good, but the fact that Ryan went behind my back to get rid of him. I guess our truce was over.

I sighed heavily and rubbed my face. "Okay, I need to find him. Maybe he didn't go far."

"I'm really sorry, Lily, I had no idea."

"No, I'm sorry I yelled, I didn't mean to be so harsh. I

apologize. It was…a shock to hear that. He's…my friend."

"Your friend? You can be friends with ghosts?"

I nodded. "Of course you can, just have to find the right one."

She was quiet for a few moments. "I'll help you find him," her voice was stronger now, "I'll make it up to you, I promise." I could hear how sorry she was, Ryan had used her. Who knows why he thought that was a good idea. There was no way I wasn't going to find out about this.

"I appreciate that, thank you." We pulled into the precinct, and I ran my ass up to Ryan's office. Thankfully, he was alone.

He looked up as I opened his door. "Roa, what can I do for you?"

I stood across from him, crossing my arms. "You told Gwen to get rid of Will?" I was proud of myself that I wasn't yelling at him, and I hoped he might recognize the calm anger of a woman.

He sighed and laced his hands on his desk. "I did. I knew you wouldn't do it, and after that last outburst, I just couldn't have him being so disruptive."

I shifted on my feet and licked my lips. "He had just found out that his brother killed him. He was upset."

Ryan's eyes softened a bit. "I see. I was unaware of the reason for his outburst. I am sorry he was upset. But he'll be better off somewhere else." Said like someone who had no idea how to deal with the dead.

"He was fine here." I started to turn, but I stopped. "I really thought things were going to be different, Ryan. I don't know why I let myself hope." And I walked back to my desk.

Gwen came running back in. "I didn't see him outside."

"Who?" Richard turned around.

I sighed and leaned against his desk. "Ryan got her to exorcize Will."

He gasped as his eyes went wide. "What!"

Her pretty face grimaced as she spoke. "I feel really bad." Gwen sat at her desk across the row from mine. "I just assumed it was another ghost that showed up like it did back east."

"Yeah, they did that at my last station as well," Richard patted my arm. "Do you know where he is?"

I shook my head. "No, not yet. Do you need me right now, or can I go ghost hunting?"

"No, you're good," I noticed he started to lean forward, likely to kiss my forehead, but he stopped. "I'll let you know if I need you."

"Thanks." He gave me a wink, and Gwen followed me out the front door. "Okay, first off, you can see him, can't you?"

She nodded. "Yes, I can see ghosts."

I took a deep breath and tried to think. "What did he look like when you were doing it? Was he in pain?" I didn't really want to know if he was in pain, I wasn't even sure if it hurt ghosts. It's not like they stuck around to be asked.

She shook her head. "No, no pain. He looked resigned and, admittedly, a little angry, but I think that was directed at Ryan. He was standing next to me like he was making sure I was doing it."

"Yeah, he's not a huge fan of Ryan's. Okay, go down the block that way, see if you can find him. I'll go this way. We'll meet back up when we're done."

"Gotcha."

———

We spent the afternoon searching for Will, but neither of us found him. I was really hoping she meant it when she didn't feel him move on. I wasn't ready for him to go. When it was time to leave for the day, I took the elevator back up to the bullpen and saw Gwen and Hyde talking by her desk and Richard sitting at his, typing away on the computer. "Guess I don't have to introduce you now," I teased as I sat down.

Gwen smiled. "No, he did it himself." I turned to them and crossed my arms. It was something I was surprised I had to practice at now.

"What do you think Hyde, wanna witch as a partner?"

He nodded, hooking his thumbs into his bulletproof vest. "I never thought I'd partner with someone who wasn't a cop, but I think I'm up for it."

"Good! Mention it to," I sighed. I didn't want to say his name. "You know, *him*," I motioned over to Ryan's office. "I don't know if he has any plans already, but if he doesn't, he'll get you started." They both nodded and walked over to the Major's office.

"Find him?" Richard turned, and I could see a hint of worry in his eyes. It was probably more for me than the missing specter.

"No." I rubbed my face. "I still can't believe he told her to do that."

He stretched his leg over and tapped my foot with his. "Was she sorry?"

"Oh yeah, I might have scared her a bit with my reaction, but I think we're good. She had no idea, I believe that." I turned back to my computer and logged out. "Might as well head home."

"Yeah, I got court in the morning, so I gotta go to bed early."

I turned back to him, my jaw on the floor. "Court on a Saturday?" I was looking forward to him spending the night. No wonder he hadn't mentioned ravishing my body tonight. Once again, the universe was against us.

"Yeah, it happens, but not often." I could hear how disappointed he was, and I didn't blame him.

"Boo." He chuckled as he logged out, and we walked over to the elevator. I peeked over at Ryan's office before the elevator door closed, and he was shaking hands with Hyde. I took that to be a good sign.

———

I swear it was the longest car ride back to my apartment. "I can't believe I couldn't find Will." I flopped on my couch, and Richard locked the door behind him.

"He'll show up, I know it." He sat next to me, and I wrapped my arms around him.

"I swear that was the only reason he hired another witch."

He kissed my forehead and hugged me tighter. "Who knows. You do need help, but I wouldn't put it past him to have an ulterior motive." Richard sighed. "Don't forget to eat something. Recovering takes strength."

"Okay," I looked up and kissed him. "Soon."

The corner of his mouth tilted in a smile. "Soon." He gave me a kiss that made me wish soon was now and headed out. I started wondering how long you should be with someone before you move in with them. I had never lived with anyone but family, but living with Richard sounded increasingly appealing. I turned to the kitchen and resigned myself to some soup for dinner when Will appeared in the middle of the room.

"I knew it!" He yelled at me, a smile on his face, pointing an accusatory finger in my direction.

I gasped and ran over to him. "Will, are you okay?" He looked worn out for a dead guy, his eyes were tired, but he nodded and put his finger away.

"I'm all right. I didnae see ya at the precinct when that purple witch was banishin' me."

I shook my head and stood in front of him. "I had no idea he asked Gwen to do that until this morning. She feels awful about that. But we looked for you all day. I was worried she made you move on."

A mischievous smile appeared on his face. "You dinnae want me to go?"

I scoffed and moved back into the kitchen. "I know you're dead and probably want to rest, but I'm selfish." I turned as I pulled a can of soup out of the cabinet. "I still want you here."

"Naw," he leaned on the counter. "I don't want to rest, I like it here." He turned and laid his back along the counter. "I think I'll stay."

My eyebrows disappeared into my hair when I heard him say that. "What, here?"

"Yeah! Think about it, Hen," he turned around and started pacing. "I can keep other ghosts out, so you aren't surprised." Okay, that did sound appealing. "I can help if something bad happens'," I wondered how he'd mess with that member of the Order who broke into my apartment last year. I opened the can of soup, and another of those pains rippled down my arm, and I cradled it against my stomach with a gasp.

"Ooh," he came running over and laid his hand on my arm, and the pain went away. "And I can be your personal healer when you need it."

I scoffed. "You're not healing. You're cooling. But thanks." He gave me a wink and sat on the counter. "If you stay here, we need some rules."

He smiled and wiggled on the counter. "Whatever you

want."

"One," I put the soup in a microwave safe bowl with some milk. "My bedroom is off-limits, so is my bathroom." I popped the bowl in the microwave and set it for three minutes. "That entire part of the apartment is off-limits. A girl needs her privacy."

"Understood," he said with a nod.

"Two," I leaned on the counter, my arms crossed. "When Richard is over, you leave us alone, no tickling or blowing on us. We need our alone time."

He giggled. "I can do that." He leaned down close to my face, a hand on his cheek. "Why didnae you tell me you was with him? I knew he was sweet on ya, but he kept his distance at the police station."

"I didn't want someone to overhear. We're still not sure if Ryan will make us stop seeing each other or not."

He sat up and patted my good shoulder. "Oh, fuck Ryan, you guys are good together." I laughed at that. "I'm glad for ya, Hen. You deserve to be happy."

"Thank you. Three, when Richard is over, no watching us, okay? It's gross."

He giggled. "Oh, fine. That all?"

"Yes, but I can amend them at any time."

"All right, all right," he jumped from the counter and gave my cheek a cold kiss. "Thank ya, Hen, I appreciate it."

"You're welcome." The microwave beeped, and as I stirred my soup and added the crackers. I couldn't believe how relieved I was that Will found his way here, and he was as all right as a dead guy could be. "Oh! Stay out of my witchy room. That's also off-limits." He put up his hands as he went invisible. I brought my soup to the living room and set it on the table, and felt the couch sink next to me. "So, are you okay after learning how you died?"

He sighed and reappeared on the couch next to me. "I don't know why my brother killed me, but I am. I didn't remember much of my life, but I remember them now, my family. I had forgotten. I'm glad I remember again." He looked down at me. "I'm remembering some good things, too."

I smiled, I'm glad he wasn't only remembering awful things. "Good! Would you be interested in learning more about your past?"

He sat back and crossed an ankle on his knee. "Maybe. Good stuff, at least." He looked at me for a moment. "I know I was married, but I don't know if we had any bairns."

I gave his knee a little pat. "I'll see what I can do." He gave me a nod, then went invisible, and I watched my couch rise as if someone stood up. I had a feeling he was going to walk around my bedroom while he could. As my soup was cooling, I texted Gwen and let her know I found Will, and he was all right. She sent back a GIF of a cheerleader jumping for joy and said Hyde seemed like a decent guy and thanked me for suggesting him. I sent her a thumbs up and asked her if she could have Hyde leave that book with Will in it on my desk. She said she would, and I put my phone down. I hoped I could find more good than bad when researching him. He deserved to remember good things and not just his murder.

True to his word, Will stayed out of my room (while I was in there, at least) and my bathroom while I got ready for bed. I slipped into bed and wished Richard were next to me. He was always warm, and I felt so safe with him. It was probably why I slept so well the last few nights. I turned on my back, which wasn't my favorite sleeping position, but my shoulder didn't bitch as much as that way. I could finally feel sleep start to suck me under when I felt something cold on my cheek.

"Good night, my bonny Hen," a quiet voice said before I fell asleep.

CHAPTER 4

"I can't believe you let him stay in your apartment." Nicola shook her head as we waited in line at Mabon's shop. I decided to drive myself over to the coffee shop since Richard was busy. Plus, I had to get used to driving again anyway. Thankfully, Nicola could meet me, so we figured we'd hang for a bit. It was almost eleven, so the morning crowd was gone, and we had beat the afternoon caffeine addicts as well. "You know he's going to break every rule you have." I shrugged, and I felt the difference in my right shoulder. It was odd not being able to lift it as high as the other one.

"It'll be fine." I didn't think he'd flat-out break my rules, but he'd at least bend them as far as they'd go, I had no doubt.

She looked down at me with the scrutiny of a best friend. "You like him."

I of course did not meet her stare. "He's my friend. Of course I like him."

"Naw, you fancy him." She nudged me with her elbow, teasing me.

I scoffed. "No, but you know how handsome he is. It's nice to see."

"I actually don't, I've never seen a picture of him."

Oh damn, why didn't I realize that? "Well, Hyde should leave a book on my desk, I'll show you later. Trust me, he's handsome." She laughed but suddenly stopped when we walked up to the counter, and Mabon smiled at us.

"Morning, Lily, Nicola, how are you today?" He was looking at Nicola as he spoke, and I bit my lip not to laugh.

"I'm good, you?" I was impressed at how smooth she was. I would be blushing something fierce and trying not to giggle.

"Doing well now that I got to see your pretty eyes." I could not stop my smile after I heard that.

"Mabon, you flirt," Nicola chuckled and gave his arm a playful pinch.

"What can I say? You make it easy," he winked at her. "What can I get you ladies today? Your usual Lily?"

"Yes, please."

Nicola looked up at the chalkboard, her finger on her chin. "I think I'll have a matcha tea latte, medium."

"Adventurous," he said as he typed the orders into the computer. "I'll have them right out." Again, I noticed how he smiled at Nicola, and I could have sworn her cheeks pinked up a bit.

"Thanks, Mabon." He smiled at her until we got to the end of the counter.

"Nicola," I whispered and put my arm in hers. "You should ask him on a date."

She looked down and shook her head, the corner of her lip curled in a little smile. "I can't do that."

"Of course you can! You are a strong, successful woman who should have a handsome bear shifter in her bed night after night." Her eyes went wide, and I laughed. "We could go on a double date!"

"Lily, The Exasperating Nicola?" Our eyes went wide as we looked at the girl by the counter.

"Entrancing!" Mabon came running up, waving his

hands. "That's entrancing, not exasperating, Anna, entrancing." We walked over, and Mabon handed us our drinks. "You are not exasperating." I couldn't stop the snort that came out of my nose.

"Try writing clearer," Anna grumbled and walked off.

Mabon sighed and shook his head. "Teenagers, am I right?"

Nicola chuckled. "I don't think anyone's called me entrancing before."

Mabon smiled. "It was the fanciest word I could come up with on the fly."

"Maybe you should have picked an easier word to spell," Anna said as she put a muffin into a little bag. That was our undoing as we burst out laughing.

"Thank you, Mabon," Nicola calmed down a bit. "I appreciate the compliment."

"You're most welcome." I grabbed us a little table in the back and took a sip of my iced chai. Reminded me of fall every time.

"Well, if that wasn't a meet/cute, I don't know what is. Give me one good reason you won't go out with him."

She took a sip of her drink and sighed. "A good reason? I don't have one, but—" she leaned forward. "He's huge with clothes on. Can you imagine what he'd be like naked?"

My eyes went wide. "Wait, you're afraid to date him because his dick might be too big?"

"Yes!" She hissed, and her cheeks went pink again. "That's a legitimate worry."

"Aw, Nicola," I reached over and laid a hand on her forearm. "I suppose I get that, but what if he's not, or what if you end up liking that? I would like to see you with your own sweetheart, and Mabon is as sweet as they come. Despite his bad penmanship." She snickered and took another sip of her drink. "Do you like him at all?"

She met my eyes. "He's adorable, and something tells me he'd give amazing backrubs." I smiled. "Why wouldn't I like him?"

"Nicola, if I've learned anything in the last six months, is that life is too short and that you deserve someone in your life to treat you like the Queen you are. And I think that man up there can do that."

"Really?" I nodded and patted her arm. She took a big gulp of her drink and got to her feet.

"Go get him," I whispered and turned in my chair as she walked back up to the counter. I wasn't about to miss history in the making. I watched as Mabon made a beeline for her, a huge smile on his face, and I crossed my fingers. I could tell she was talking, and when he nodded, I knew there was no turning back.

———

I drove to Richard's house after I grilled Nicola when she sat back down at the table. Where was the date, when, how'd he say yes? All the nosey questions I could think of. I swear she seemed more relaxed now that she had an answer. Her shoulders weren't as tense, and she had a little smile on her face as she talked about him. She said when she asked him for a date, she could feel her nerves going insane, but when he smiled, it calmed her down. He said, 'I'd love nothing more than to spend time with you, Nicola.' I giggled at that. It sounded like something he'd say. I really hoped they worked out. They were some of the best people in town. Tomorrow night, the four of us were going to Pizzone's and then axe throwing, which surprised me, but hey, I was up for anything.

I used my key, and when I opened the door, I saw Richard

sitting on the couch, reading a book. He was still in his dress shirt and pants, but his shoes were by the door. He looked up as I walked in and locked the door behind me.

"Hello, gorgeous." He smiled, and I gave him a kiss before sitting next to him.

"Hey, handsome, so we have a double date tomorrow night." I gave his thigh a squeeze.

He smiled mischievously. "Do we? With whom?" He asked like he already knew, it was cute.

"Nicola and Mabon."

He sat back with a smile. "Finally! That's great."

I couldn't help the giggle that leaked out. "It is. We're going to The Pizzone for dinner, then axe throwing in Woodhurst."

"Axe throwing," he laughed and crossed his arms. "Sounds like a certain shifter wants to show off."

I snickered and sat back. "It does, doesn't it? But it sounds fun. Pizzone has great calzones, and I've never been axe throwing before." I looked over at my right arm. "I think I'm going to be terrible at it, but I'm not trying to impress anyone."

He gave me a little wink. "Can't wait."

I managed to keep my cheeks from blazing at the attention. "So, how was court?"

He put his hands behind his head and leaned back on the couch. "Oh fine, I gave my testimony, and the judge charged them. Took about an hour."

"Good. I think I need to do some research tonight."

"Yeah? Need your Igor?"

I smiled and gave his knee a little nudge with my foot. "Always. But it might be boring, going through books mostly."

"Hmm, maybe Igor can make you dinner instead?"

I smiled. He was still taking care of me. "That'd be nice.

Oh, um," I slid my feet under me and laid my hand on his thigh. "I found Will."

He laid a hand on mine. He looked relieved. "Good, where was he?"

I cleared my throat. "My apartment."

His eyes went wide, and he sat back, his arms crossed. "Your apartment?"

"Mm-hmm. I gave him some rules to follow, so it should be okay." Richard was quiet for a few moments before he reached up and held my chin for a second.

"As long as it's what you want."

"It's better than him roaming around causing problems all over town."

He nodded in agreement. "All right then. I'm glad he's okay." He ran his hand through his hair. I looked at the clock on his wall and saw it was only one.

"Me too. So," without warning, I straddled his hips and wrapped my arms around his neck. "We got time?"

His arms wrapped around me, and his hands grabbed my ass perfectly. "Fuck yeah." I smiled a second before I kissed him. He squeezed my backside before I felt his hands slide under my shirt and up my back. I heard a little playful gasp from him. "No bra?"

I nipped at his lower lip. "Nope."

The chuckle that came from him radiated through me as he smiled mischievously. "You wicked little thing." His hand moved to the back of my neck and pulled me to his lips. "I'm going to touch, and kiss, and lick and nibble every," he nipped my lip, "inch of you."

"You better," I started unbuttoning his shirt. "Or I'm going to be a different kind of wicked." He chuckled, as one hand covered my breast. His hand was warm, and he rolled my nipple between two fingers. Tingles spread through me, and I sighed as I reached between us and undid his belt. I could already tell he was ready for me, but I knew he was going to take his time. I was not going to complain. I whipped his belt off him and tossed it in the room and unbuttoned his pants. It was harder than I thought it would be. His hand was being really distracting. His other arm pulled me close, and he kissed me deeply, as he laid me back against the couch. I kept my legs around him and kicked off my shoes.

They landed with a ridiculously loud thud on the hardwood floor, and I giggled as he moved to my neck. His lips were soft as he gently sucked that sensitive skin below my ear. I couldn't stop the little moan as I reached between us and squeezed him. He felt thick in my hand, and I knew he'd feel amazing in me. His head lifted as he moaned at my touch, his eyes closed for a moment.

"Does that feel good?" I whispered.

"So good," he leaned down and nipped my earlobe. I managed to pull his pants off with my feet, and it made him laugh. That sound, that happy, joyful noise, gave me so much peace. "Impressive."

"Right?" He stood, and I quickly found myself in his arms as he carried me to the bedroom. He had one of those amazing beds that was huge and comfortable, just the perfect amount of support.

Richard stopped at the foot of the bed. "I kind of want to toss you on it, but I don't want to hurt your arm."

I smiled. "I'll be okay." I gave him a kiss, and I felt him lift me a little higher before I fell through the air onto the bed. I gave a little shriek before I landed on my butt, laughing. He would definitely be doing that to me again. He was still at the end of the bed, smiling at me, and I got to admire him in a half-unbuttoned dress shirt and boxer briefs. "You are so beautiful."

His hungry eyes softened a bit as he finished unbuttoning his shirt. "You are beautiful, and I feel lucky to be in your life like this." His shirt fell to the floor, and he crawled onto the bed over to me. "Like me moving here was fate." His hand slowly ran up my leg to the zipper and button on my jeans. I looked down as his fingers undid the button and pulled the zipper down. He got up on his knees and pulled my pants off in one swift movement that made me giggle.

I took my shirt off and threw it somewhere nearby, and there we both were, in bed in nothing but our underwear. Not that being in our underwear in bed was an unusual thing, but it meant more this time. He crawled up the bed, and I let him settle between my legs. I could feel how hard he was, and I sighed at the sensation as he pressed himself against me. He kissed my forehead, then my brow and my temple, then my cheeks.

"I don't think I've ever said this while I was completely conscious," I chuckled as he kissed the tip of my nose. "But I love you, Lily." He looked me in the eyes as he said that, and there was nothing but truth and love in them. "You are the most wonderful woman I've ever known. You're smart and powerful and beautiful."

I smiled and gave him a kiss as my hands ran up and down his back. "I love you too, Richard. I've never met a man that cared so much for others, or me for that matter. I feel lucky to have you, too." He gave me another kiss and then moved to my neck, his teeth gently biting that sensitive skin as he moved down my chest. I opened my arms and watched as he kissed over one breast and then over to the other. Giving special attention to my already hardened nipples as he drew them between his teeth.

I couldn't stop my legs from running up and down his side as he did that. The feel of his lips and teeth made me tremble with every movement. He moved down to my stomach, and it twitched at his touch.

He chuckled. "Ticklish?" And kissed my stomach again.

"Maybe a little." He moved to my hip and slowly pulled my underwear down, kissing where it once was. He pulled them down my legs like he did a few days ago, then kissed the top of my foot. "You really meant every inch, didn't you?" He looked up at me and winked as he moved to my ankle and then my calf. His hand gripped my thigh, and his thumb made little circles on the inside of it. That sensation surprised me, it felt soft, and it was so close to my middle that the tease about it was driving me insane. "Fuck Richard if you don't touch me—" I couldn't finish my sentence as he pounced.

His face was between my legs, and that amazing tongue was slowly licking my clit. It felt even more amazing than the other day, like he knew he could take his time, and I watched him feast on me. The sensation was maddening, and I could feel myself getting wetter with every lick. I've never had anyone pay so much attention to that part of my body. I knew there were women who liked this, and now I could see why. I laid my head back and sighed, letting myself enjoy every lick of his tongue when I realized his fingers were also sliding up the inside of my thigh.

"Yes," I breathed. "Yes, Richard, touch me," I said a moment before he slid a finger inside me. I gasped as he rubbed on a spot inside that made what he was doing with his tongue even more distracting. His lips pressed against me as the licking was replaced with sucking, and I felt myself press against him. The sensation was amazing. Near constant pleasure rocked my body as I buried my hands in his hair, holding him there. I felt him moan against me as I started riding his finger. That wonderful pressure started building inside me, and I knew I wouldn't last long. "Don't stop," I begged him, and he sucked deeper. I couldn't stop the moan that fled my lips as the orgasm broke inside me, wave after wave of pleasure spread through my body.

I looked down as he raised his head. His lips were glistening, and I watched as he pulled that finger from inside me and put it in his mouth, sucking me from his skin. "Fuck you're good at that." I couldn't stop myself, and he smiled.

"I think you liked that." His voice was low, and I smiled as he crawled back up to me, once again kissing as he went.

"I think you did, too." He smiled and laid next to me, kissing my shoulder when I noticed. "Good sir, you still have clothes on."

He still hadn't shed his boxer briefs and chuckled. "I forgot." He started to reach for them when I grabbed his wrist.

"Let me." He laid back, his hands going behind his head, watching me like I watched him, the corner of his mouth tilted up. I slid down his muscular body and rubbed my cheek along that hardness that was still trapped in his boxer briefs. "How haven't you just busted a hole through these." He laughed as I lifted the elastic band over him and watched as he spilled from them, hard and thick. I slid his underwear down his legs and tossed them somewhere behind me. His dick was as thick as I felt the other day, and I let him watch me as I kissed up his leg. The closer I got to him, I could feel the heat he radiated. "Damn." I looked up at him, the way he looked at me, the heat in his eyes made my body respond. "I don't suppose you'd mind if I wanted to kiss *you* all over?"

"My body is yours," he purred, and I smiled. I scooted closer to him, and my tongue ran along the underside of his dick. He moaned, and I felt his hips twitch a little under me. "God damn, you're sexy Lily." I chuckled and kissed down the side of his dick down to the inside of his thigh, paying special attention to those lovely hip dips. As I kissed his stomach, my hand ran up his leg and wrapped my fingers around his dick. He moaned as I gently squeezed and moved my hand up and down. "Oh, you wicked little thing." I looked up, and he was biting his lower lip, his eyes closed in pleasure.

"I'm *your* wicked little thing," I said and straddled his hips. His eyes flashed open as he sat forward, his arms going around me. "And I want you inside me." He held himself still as I lowered myself down onto him, both of us gasping at the sensation. He stretched me perfectly, and the more of him I put inside, the more he rubbed on some hidden spot no one had ever touched before. He laid his head on my shoulder as his arms held me up.

"Oh, fuck Lily, you feel fucking exquisite." He kissed my neck, and I slowly started moving my hips. The feel of him inside me was perfection. I could barely think because his dick felt so good in me, I wanted more. I wanted all of him. I moved faster as his hand ran up my torso and covered my breast. I watched as he held it up and took my sensitive nipple in his mouth, sucking on all that glorious pink skin. I felt his tongue run along it while his teeth gently bit my skin. The shock was pleasant, and I rolled my hips faster. That newly discovered place in me was getting rubbed over and over. I couldn't stop the moans coming out of me.

He let go of my nipple and pulled my lips to his, and he kissed me fiercely, like he was claiming me, and I let him. His tongue swept into my mouth, his lips pressed against mine, and we held each other there, kissing as I rode him. One of his hands stayed on my back while the other slid down and squeezed my ass. That little pressure felt amazing, and I moaned into his mouth. He let go, and I was honestly a little disappointed, but not for long as I felt his hand between us, and his fingers rubbed on my clit.

"Oh, fuck who's wicked now." I managed to say. He laughed, and I rode him faster, harder. The feel of him inside and outside was an assault on my senses in a way I never knew I wanted. "Oh fuck," I said over and over. I knew I was close. I could feel that orgasm building inside me. "Fuck I'm close," I whispered. Knowing that I would feel this way again with him, was comforting.

"Let it happen, baby," he moaned. "I want to feel you come on my —" He couldn't even get the sentence out before that pleasure broke inside me with a fury I had never felt before. I yelled his name as I felt myself squeeze around him as my body felt the most perfect release I had ever experienced. "Oh, fuck Lily!" He moaned, and I felt him thrust upwards, hard.. His arms held me tight against him as his moans radiated through me. My arms stayed around him as my hand ran lazily through his hair. I didn't want to let him go. Ever.

———

An hour later, we were still in bed, under the covers. I ran my hand up and down his bare chest as he talked about nothing and everything. How his favorite baseball team was doing, the rumors I'd been hearing around town, nothing exciting, but I loved it. I scooted closer to him, and he suddenly rolled on top of me.

I laughed as he settled between my legs. "I don't know

about you, but I'm itching for round two."

I smiled. "Really?"

"Abso-fucking-lutely." We spent hours in bed, just like he said he wanted to do. He rubbed my feet, and his fingers brought me pleasure again. I massaged his back and sucked that glorious dick of his. Over and over, we brought each other pleasure. When we got hungry, he ordered pizza, and we sat naked in bed, eating and watching horror movies. It was the best fucking afternoon. Literally.

CHAPTER 5

Richard and I spent a great deal of the day in bed, kissing, talking, and, you know, everything else you do in bed with someone you love. I had never had so many orgasms in a twenty-four-hour period before. I decided that the research I needed to do that night wasn't as important as staying in bed with him. One night wouldn't hurt. I drove back to my apartment the next afternoon to get ready for our double date with Nicola and Mabon. Richard would come pick me up in a few hours, and I couldn't wait. I just wanted to be with him. He was so soothing and strong. No one had ever made me so happy, and I don't think I'd ever fallen so fast for anyone before. Not that anyone else deserved to be fallen for that fast. Richard really was one of a kind. I walked into my apartment and threw my purse on the couch as Will appeared behind it.

"Where ya been, my bonny Hen?" He crossed his arms like a discerning parent, and I laughed.

"With Richard."

"Ooh, Richard," he slid down the back of the couch and landed with his head on his hand, stretched out along it. "I suppose I approve."

I scoffed and walked into my bedroom. "Like I need your approval."

"You never know," I heard his footsteps walk over to the bedroom door before he leaned on the doorframe. "He could be one of those crooked cops. I need to look out for ya." I could hear the tease in his voice and shook my head.

"Crooked is one thing he is not," I pulled a dark purple tank and some black leggings out of my drawer and threw them on the bed. "He is amazing and —" My arm erupted in pain, and I hissed as I cradled it against me. Along with the annoying electrical zap, it felt like my forearm had a charlie horse. "Ow ow ow fuck fuck fuck!"

"Oh goodness." Will appeared next to me and held my arm. "This seems different."

"Yeah," I said through gritted teeth. His cold hands rubbed my forearm until the muscle relaxed. I had never had a charlie horse in my arm before, and it's not any more pleasant than ones in your calf, I'll tell you that. I caught my breath and gave my arm one last rub. "Thanks."

"You're welcome, my bonny Hen." He walked out of the room and leaned on the doorframe again. "You look like you're leaving again."

"Yeah, gonna take a quick shower, then Richard's picking me up. We have a double date tonight with Nicola and Mabon."

He gasped, a huge smile on his face. "The doc's got herself a date, huh? Well, good for her. Who's Mabon?" I opened the bathroom door and turned the shower on. Being an older building, it took time for the water to heat up.

"Owns a coffee shop in town," I called back.

"Ah, she'll love that." I got a towel and threw it on the toilet. "Why you smilin' Hen?"

When he said that, I realized I was, and it went away. "I can't smile?"

"No, you can, but you don't usually smile at nothing. Whatcha thinkin' about?" Again, he was teasing me something fierce. I crossed my arms and stared him down. "Would it be the giant Dick that puts such a pretty smile on that face?"

My eyes went wide at that. "Excuse me!"

He walked over to me and pitched my cheeks. "Richard! That man is huge!" His fingers were cold like always, but I managed not to smile.

"What if it was? And can you please not call him Dick, that's weird."

He laughed and sat on the bed. "I'm happy for ya Hen. You've had some dafty men the last few years. This one, I think he'll stick."

I bit the inside of my lip to keep my smile under wraps. "Oh yeah?"

"Yeah."

I nodded, my arms still crossed. "I think so, too." I started to turn to the bathroom but stopped. "You're not supposed to be in my room."

"We're just talkin!" I watched him flop back on my bed as I shut the door. I didn't really mind if he was in my room while we talked, but I knew I'd have to remind him of my rules every so often and held in my giggle at his reaction.

———

When it was time for the date, Richard picked me up and drove us to The Pizzone. It was a newer place on the other side of town, but it was proving to be a welcome addition. We arrived right when Mabon and Nicola did and waited by the front door. I watched as Mabon opened the car door for her, and I could tell she was trying not to giggle as she got out and took his arm. Nicola was almost six foot herself, but even in heels, Mabon was still a few inches taller. I looked up at Richard, then back to them, and sighed.

"I look like a child out with my parents."

Richard laughed and put his arm around me. "No, you don't." He kissed my forehead as they stopped in front of us.

"Is she complaining about being short?" Nicola teased, and Mabon laughed as Richard pulled open the door.

"Is it complaining when there's truly nothing you can do about it?" They laughed as we walked inside. The smell of pizza hit my nose and made my stomach grumble. Sausages and sauces and fresh baked bread, I had a feeling everything on the menu was going to be good. "Mmm, smells good." I hadn't eaten much that day, nor had Richard, since we had just spent most of the morning in bed with each other, so I knew we were going to just inhale whatever we ordered.

The hostess smiled as we walked up. "Hello, welcome to Pizzone, four?"

"Yes, please," Richard answered, and I took his arm like Nicola had Mabon's, and we followed her to a table by the front window.

"Enjoy!" We all sat down, Nicola and Richard flanked me, and the waiter walked up with some water.

"Welcome in, I'm Josh. I'll be your server tonight. Shall we start with drinks?" The men ordered beers, and I got a pop, and Nicola stuck with water.

"I don't think I've ever been here." I watched Nicola look around. The restaurant was very red, like most Italian-esque places. Red plastic cups, red and white checkered tablecloths, the works.

"I like their ham and cheese calzone," Mabon said. "Cheesy and salty, and the bread is soft and garlicky. Do you like pizza?" I turned to Richard and tried to hide my smile as Mabon talked to Nicola.

"I do. I've never had a calzone, though. I thought I'd try that tonight." She reached out and laid her hand on Mabon's, and I watched the smile on his face brighten the room.

"Good choice." Josh brought our drinks, and we ordered. Mabon got his favorite calzone, Nicola got a vegetable calzone, which we could all agree we hadn't tried. I got a small pizza with black olives, and Richard got a meatball stromboli, which, when I saw the picture, I kind of regretted my choice. It looked amazing. Oh well, next time.

Nicola turned to Mabon, "So, where are you from?" I reached under the table and laid my hand on Richard's knee, and he laid his hand on mine. I watched as Mabon and Nicola talked and got to know each other. I noticed how she was smiling at him. It wasn't her typical flirty smile with the corner of her mouth tilted. It was soft, and her eyes were roaming over him every so often. Josh brought our food, but Mabon still paid attention to Nicola, being the sweetest date I'd ever seen. Laughing full and happy at her jokes and giving her little touches on the shoulder or arm.

I felt Richard lean over, and I met his lean. "I think it's going well," he whispered.

I gave him a little kiss." I agree.

"So, how did you two get together?" I heard Mabon ask, and we turned to him. Nicola had her head resting in her hand, smiling at us. She knew exactly what happened, but I guess she didn't tell him.

"Well," I glanced at Richard, who gave me the floor. "My old partner Howard gave him my number. When he was murdered, Richard and I started working together to find the killer."

Mabon 'tsk'd.' "I remember that, it was sad. Howard used

to come in every Saturday for drinks." I smiled at that, I didn't know he frequented Mabon's shop like that.

"We started working together exclusively after that," Richard continued. "I really liked spending time with her, no matter what we were doing. She was so pretty and smart, and honestly, I couldn't wait to see her every day."

I smiled and touched his cheek. "We kept sending memes and funny videos to each other." Richard laughed. "When I woke up in the hospital after the Fells died, I didn't remember much about the week before. But I knew there was something important I was forgetting."

"Did you remember what it was?" Mabon snickered.

I nodded and took Richard's hand. "Our first kiss."

Mabon's eyes went wide. "You forgot your first kiss?"

Richard chuckled. "To be fair, we were under attack, and she lost her arm soon after. But she remembered eventually."

"It was quite a kiss. I think it was a week or two after I woke, I was about to be discharged, and he offered to take me home. I was sitting on the hospital bed, and he was putting my shoes on for me."

He laughed. "Those awful crocs that Nicola got you."

I laughed, and Nicola playfully gasped. "Excuse me, but they were the easiest shoes for her to get on by herself! It's not my fault they were neon green." Mabon laughed and gave her hand a pat.

"He put those ugly things on my feet, and I thanked him. And he said, 'No thanks needed, that's what boyfriends do.'" He smiled and kissed my cheek.

"Oh, he snuck in there, did he?" Mabon laughed.

"He certainly did. I teased him, 'You're my boyfriend now?'"

Richard kissed my hand. "And I said, 'If you'll have me'."

"And I kissed him. Best decision I ever made."

Nicola sighed. "So sweet."

"I think I got lucky." I gave Richard a wink and went back to my thankfully extremely good pizza.

———

Before we left, Nicola dragged me to the restroom and leaned against the closed door.

"I'm so angry at myself for not asking him out earlier," she smiled. "He's just the sweetest."

"I told you!" I walked over to the sink and washed my hands. The pizza was amazing but was a bit messy, and I didn't trust myself to have gotten all the sauce off them.

"I really want to go home with him tonight," she giggled.

"I don't think he'll hate that idea." I dried my hands. "Oh! Speaking of going home," I made sure we were alone because there's nothing more embarrassing than gushing around strangers. "Richard and I finally slept together."

Her eyes went wide as she gasped. "Oh my god, tell me everything!" She gripped my arms and hopped a little. I gave her the abbreviated version about how he was just as amazing in bed as out. "It's about time. It's been a long while for you, hasn't it?"

"Yep."

She crossed her arms. "Did you use protection?"

I laughed, and she couldn't pretend to be serious anymore. "I'm on the pill, and we both got tested last month. We're okay."

"All right, as long as you trust him."

I nodded. "I don't think I've ever trusted anyone so much before."

She opened the door for me and smiled. "I'm so glad you guys are working out, you deserve that hunky man in your bed."

"And you deserve that giant teddy bear in yours." She gave me a wink, and we walked from the bathroom to the parking lot and joined our men.

Mabon chuckled when he saw us walking over. "Oh, I know that look," he teased, and Nicola took his hand. "What are you two talking about?" He asked and gave her cheek a kiss. I saw the smile on her face as he lingered for just a moment. I don't think I'd ever seen her so happy.

"Nothing," we said at the same time.

Richard laughed. "I think I can take a guess." He gave me a long, sweet kiss, and I wrapped my arms around him.

I heard Mabon chuckle. "Don't they look cozy?" I chuckled and kissed Richard's cheek.

"I like to think so."

————

Twenty minutes later, we were at Solstice Axe Throwing. The place was hopping for a Sunday night, so I assumed they did good business. Thankfully, Mabon thought ahead and reserved a lane for us. We listened to the employee, who was dressed like a lumberjack, complete with a red flannel shirt, suspenders, and hiking boots, give a safety spiel, and then we were left to our own devices for forty-five minutes. Like gentlemen, the boys let us go first. I picked up one of the axes and handed it to Nicola.

"Good luck." I winked at her, and she gave me a sly smile. She stepped up to the end of the lane and raised the axe, and with a mighty heave, threw it down to the target and hit the dead middle.

"Damn!" Mabon laughed and clapped as she did a little celebration dance, and I handed her the next one. We watched as she threw the axe right next to the first one. Mabon's jaw dropped as I handed her the last one, and once again, it hit the middle. "I think I'm in love." Mabon walked over to her and wrapped his big arms around her waist. "That was incredible."

"It was, wasn't it?" Now, it was my turn for my jaw to drop as she kissed him. A sweet lips only kiss that I knew was driving Mabon wild.

I felt Richard next to my ear. "You sneaky little witch." He was chuckling and put his arms around me.

"What me?" I turned and held his face. "Maybe." I kissed him deeply, and I waved at Mabon to just go before me. When I finally came up for air, I saw he had done the exact same thing. Nicola looked over at me, but I shook my head. "Wasn't me."

She looked at Mabon, a little crooked smile on her face. "Impressive." He was smiling, but I noticed he looked behind us, and his smile disappeared. "What?" We all turned, but whatever he was looking at wasn't evident.

He scratched his beard and turned to talk to us. "I didn't expect to see him out, honestly. The guy with the dark hair by the bar, his name's Olin. His wife and brother recently passed, and he wasn't doing too well." I looked to where Mabon had indicated. There was indeed a man in his mid-thirties with dark hair nursing a beer as he sat on a picnic table. "I guess it's a good thing he's out and about now."

"How long ago did they pass?" Nicola asked as she put a hand on his shoulder.

"She died about six months ago," my heart broke a little for him. "His brother about four months ago."

"Shit." I breathed out and felt Richard's hand on my back.

"Yeah. Woodhurst has a big wolf pack, so he's not alone for long. But a lot of us shifters in the area have been checking up on him, making sure he's okay. I'm glad he's out of the house, though." He waved, and the mourning man noticed and walked over with a head bob.

Mabon held out his hand, and Olin shook it. "Nice to see you out, Olin."

"Nice to be out." He looked at the three of us. "Different crowd than you usually hang with Mabon." The smile on his face didn't reach his eyes. I had never seen such a look of sorrow in anyone's eyes before. It almost hurt to look at him.

Mabon chuckled. "I'm on a date," he held out his hand toward Nicola, who took it and joined his side. "This is Dr. Nicola Stroud, Nicola, this is Olin York."

She shook his hand. "Nice to meet you."

"And you."

Mabon turned to us. "And this is Detective Richard Moss and his girlfriend, Lily Roa. She hates my coffee," he teased.

Olin chuckled and shook our hands. "To be fair, I hate all coffee."

"Fair enough." My magic tingled as I shook his hand as it recognized a shifter. Made sense since Mabon told us the shifter community was helping him through this tough time. But as I looked at him, the shape of him got my attention. It looked familiar. How tall he was, how wide his shoulders were. I had been keeping my little onyx rock with me ever since the Glass murder, and I mentally patted myself on the back for that. Because as I put my hand in my pocket, I could feel the rock vibrating slightly. Was this our guy? He wasn't fae at all, so I wondered where it was coming from. "Hope you don't mind, I saw Mabon, and I wanted to say hi."

"The more the merrier!" The big shifter said with a smile.

"Absolutely," Richard picked up an axe. "Want a go?" I smiled at how sweet he was, inviting a stranger to join us so he didn't have to be alone.

"Oh no, I'm just here 'cause it's noisy. Keeps my brain from wandering." Knowing about his past, I understood that. Mabon handed Nicola one of the axes, and she took her turn, a little less spectacularly this time, but it was clear he didn't care as he gave her cheek a little celebration kiss when she was done.

"This your first time here?" Olin asked us and took a drink of his beer.

"Yeah, never threw an axe before. It might be harder than I realize." I reached up and held the crystal around my neck. From the vibrating rock, it was clear that there was some kind of fae magic around him, but it wasn't compulsion. He wasn't glowing at all. I walked behind him to set my drink down, and Richard kept him talking. I kept hold of my crystal and cast a small spell to tell me what I sensed, and it slammed into me. My head throbbed, and I had to steady myself against the table.

It was a bond, a powerful one that was clearly put there by a fae. The kind of bond that a fae could work their own magic through. The kind of bond that a fae could make a person do whatever they wanted, and magic wouldn't see it as a compulsion. It was just the fae doing what they wanted to do. Poor Olin was really wrapped up in something bad.

I felt a hand on my shoulder. "You all right?" I looked up at Nicola. She looked a little worried.

"I'm fine, yeah." I saw Olin was still talking with Richard. He hadn't noticed my reaction. Olin shook hands with Mabon once more and walked back to the bar. I took one of the axes, and Richard stood next to me. I leaned close to his ear and whispered. "Olin has a spell on him. A fae bound him to them."

"That doesn't sound good." I threw the axe as well as my left arm could, and I was just glad it didn't bounce off the target and hit the floor.

"No, it's not."

———

When our time was up, we turned in the axes. Olin was still by the bar, but didn't look like he had gotten another drink. Mabon waved bye to him, and we walked to our cars.

"Well, I don't know about you," Mabon turned to Nicola, her hand in his. "But I could go for a nightcap. Join me?"

"Absolutely." She turned back to me. "I'll see you tomorrow."

"All right, be safe." She gave me a hug while the men did their manly handshake, and we got in our respective cars. "You know I'd be more happy, glowy about how well it went between them if we didn't meet Olin tonight. I think he might be our guy."

He sighed and started for my apartment. "I concur."

"The shape of him just seemed familiar, the height and width and that spell on him? I can't help but wonder." I sighed and pulled out my phone and texted Gwen what I learned. "Maybe our new witch can look into it as well."

"Good idea." I looked over and saw Richard smiling at nothing.

"What are you smiling at?" I teased him and laid a hand on his leg.

"Just thinking how wonderful and normal tonight was, two couples out having fun." He looked over at me. "We should do it more often."

"I agree. Now that I'm not stuck in that horrible sling, I think it'll be more fun."

"Good, I can't wait to show off my beautiful girlfriend." He lifted my hand and gave it a kiss.

"I can't wait to be shown off."

CHAPTER 6

I woke in Richard's arms and smiled. I couldn't help but think about the last few nights and how everything he did felt amazing. How he listened to me and my body and changed whatever he needed to. I'd never been with someone so in tune with me before.

I rolled over, and he opened his eyes. "Morning." His voice was quiet, but I could still feel the sound rumble through me.

"Morning." I ran my hand through his sleep-tousled hair. "Hungry?"

A mischievous smile spread along his lips. "Starving." He flipped me on top of him, and I squealed at the sudden movement. "I think I need an appetizer." I kissed him deep as his hands cupped my ass. I could feel his own body reacting to the stimuli, which was easily done since we had gone to sleep naked. I sat up, that wonderful, warm hardness pressed against me. He moaned and sat up. His teeth immediately took a nipple in his mouth, and I lifted up just a bit and slowly sank down onto him. His groan radiated from where he held me in his mouth and through my body. He still felt amazing in me, and as I moved, he rubbed that spot inside me that only he could.

His arms held me tight against him as I moved, I needed to feel all of him, and I pressed him to me. His lips kissed my collarbone when my orgasm surprised me, and I cried out as I squeezed around him over and over. He joined me a moment later, his cry echoing in his room. I ran my hand through his hair as my body had little spasms around him.

"Mm, morning orgasm before work, I don't think I've had one of those."

Richard laughed as his hands ran up and down my back. "Me either."

———

When we got to the precinct, I saw that Hyde had left that book on my desk. I picked it up and made the excuse that I had to ask Nicola something about the bodies and took the elevator down to the morgue. The door opened, and I turned towards her desk and saw her typing something on the computer.

"Nicola!" I whisper yelled, and she jumped as she turned to me. Her eyes squinted as I quickly sat in the chair next to her, laying the book on her desk.

"You're in a cheeky mood."

I leaned close just in case anyone could hear. "Tell me everything."

Nicola smiled and leaned close. "Well, we went back to his shop for a drink. He showed me how he made his coffee. He was so sweet, and I had so much fun. We ended up making out in the kitchen." I giggled at her. "He's such a good kisser, and his hands, god, his hands felt so good."

"So, there's gonna be a second date?" I asked hopefully.

She bit her lower lip as she nodded. "Most definitely."

I squealed and held her hands. "Yay, I can't wait to hear all about them."

"Well, I expect to hear all about your dates with Richard. I guess now you're going to go out more now your arm isn't all stuck to your chest?"

I chuckled. "Yeah, I think that's the plan. I can't wait to spend time with him outside of my apartment. Well, I can't wait to spend more time in my apartment, if you know what I mean."

She laughed and crossed her arms. "You were right. We both deserve these sweet, brilliant men. In our lives and our beds."

"Damn right, we do."

She sighed happily and pointed at the book. "What's that?"

I patted the cover. "That book I told you Hyde found." I quickly flipped through it and found the picture of Will and his brothers. "Here he is." I pointed to Will, and her jaw dropped.

"You've been holding out on me, Lily." I laughed as she took the book and read a bit. "I mean, you said he was handsome, but damn."

"I'm going to tell him you said that."

She snickered. "Feel free." She clicked her tongue and shook her head. "Why on earth would his brother kill him?"

I shrugged. "Don't know, it looks like he beat him in the head with a hammer or something. It's on the back of his head, so he probably didn't see it coming."

"Probably not." She turned to her computer and started typing something on her computer. Her eyes scanned the screen for a moment, then clicked on something else. "Here it is."

"Here what is?" I scooted around and leaned on her desk to see what she had found. "Is that—"

"His death report." It was old, yellow, and most likely scanned in, so it was difficult to read.

"Holy shit. You have access to records that far back?"

"I do." She put her finger on the screen to help her read. "William McKay, aged thirty-five, died of blunt force trauma to the back of the head."

I snorted. "No shit. God, he was so young."

"Poor guy." She skimmed the screen and kept reading. "The victim and suspect, his younger brother Ruben, had gotten into a fight over a woman." As the words fled her lips, something inside me told me that couldn't be true. I knew he was married, and I had a sneaking suspicion that he was head over heels in love with his wife. "Ruben claimed his brother was trying to steal his wife while the victim insisted he wasn't and tried to leave a party they were at. The suspect picked up a rock hammer and attacked the victim, striking him once in the back of the head. Death was most likely instantaneous. Ruben was arrested on site and awaits trial."

"I'd believe that." I stood straight and gasped as Nicola scrolled down and revealed a photo of Will on a morgue table. His eyes were closed, and a blanket covered him from the navel down. I thanked my lucky stars it was a black and white photo. "Oh my god."

"Damn sorry, I didn't think that was there."

"It's okay, I've seen worse." I was surprised at how upset looking at that photo made me. It was like seeing a friend at their funeral. Nicola scrolled down a little more.

"They attached his obituary as well." I leaned closer and read it. William Evander McKay was murdered this past Saturday, the twenty-sixth of May, by his brother Ruben McKay. He leaves behind his beloved wife, Rhoswen McKay, and their five children, Alister, Iain, Arabella, Lachlan, and Thomas. I stopped reading then. I knew he was married. He remembered he was married as well, but here were the names of his children. All five of them.

"Are you going to tell him?" Nicola looked up at me.

"I think he'd like to know." Because looking at those names, I had a feeling that I'd want to know as well.

I walked back up the stairs, hugging the book as those names floated through my mind. I thought about how I'd break it to Will, that he did have children, five in fact. I sat at my desk and turned to Richard. He was sitting with his back to me, typing on his computer. Something so ordinary, but my heart leapt at the sight of him, and the sadness of what I had just learned was put at the back of my mind.

He finished typing and turned to me, leaning close. "How'd the rest of their date go?" He asked quietly.

I giggled at how he was just as invested as I was. "They made out in the kitchen of his shop."

He laughed and sat back. "Good, I'm glad they finally got together."

"Me too." My eyes drifted over to his coat rack as those names roamed through my mind again.

Richard leaned a little closer. "Hey, you okay?" I looked back over to him, concern on his face. "You look a little... haunted."

"I do?" He nodded. "Probably because of this." I pulled the printout of Will's obituary and handed it to him. He sat back and read it.

When he was done, his free hand rubbed the back of his neck. "Fuck."

"Yeah." I watched his eyes read it again. "He knows he was married, but he didn't know if he had any children."

He handed the paper back to me, and I put it in my pocket. "You going to show him?"

I nodded. "Yeah. I'd want to know."

He patted my knee. "Same." Richard sighed and turned back to his desk. "Well, Jordan Glass's attorney had some questions for you," he grabbed a business card off his desk, then swiveled around and handed it to me. "You can just email him, then he'll send you the questions."

"Alrighty, I'll get on that. Then I have my first physical therapy at two."

He nodded. "Do you need me to take you?"

I thought for a moment. "I don't know, I don't think so?"

"Maybe I should drive you just in case they work you out and you're in pain afterwards." I smiled and tried to hide it behind my hand. That kind of smile was full of love and appreciation, which wasn't meant for work.

"That's not a bad idea, thank you." He gave me a little wink and turned back to his computer.

———

Thankfully, I finished typing up my answers for the lawyer before lunch because I did not want to go to physical therapy on an empty stomach. Now that I was official, my testimony mattered more. I was an expert witness, and boy, did that attorney have a lot of questions. I was trying not to take offense since I had the same expert evidence when I was just a consultant. But I had never gotten so many questions before a trial, and I could see now that my position was being taken more seriously than before. I was glad because Jordan would need a good defense. While technically guilty, he hadn't been in his right mind, and trials like this were still controversial. I made sure to include the love I felt from that spell I did on his girlfriend's phone and that, in my expert opinion, no one who loved the victim like that would willingly kill her.

Thankfully, Sal's wasn't busy, so we both wolfed down a burger and made it to the physical therapists with ten minutes to spare. I checked in at the desk, and we sat in some chairs in a big, open room full of workout equipment. People of all ages were stepping over things or lifting them. Two people rode bikes, and one was walking slowly on a treadmill.

"Lily Roa?" I heard a female voice call my name, and I looked over to the desk. A young woman around my age with curly blonde hair was looking around at those of us who were in the waiting area.

"That's me." I patted Richard's knee and stepped up to her. Her eyes roamed over me a moment, lingering on my non-slinged up arm.

She looked down at the paperwork in her hand. "Arm reattachment at the shoulder?" She looked back up, clearly confused.

"Yep!" I pulled the side of my shirt down and showed her my scar.

She pointed at it. "Yep! Okay, well, follow me, and we'll get you started." I gave her a nod and followed her over to a room that had a treatment table in it. You know, the kind, just high enough you have to jump up to get on, and the soft bits are not quite soft enough. I hopped up on it, and she sat on a tall stool that moved around on wheels and pulled up a moving trey table thing with a laptop on it. "I'm Avis," she held out her hand, and I gave it a shake. "And I can honestly say I didn't expect you to be out of your sling yet. How long has it been?"

"Six months and ten days. The surgeon said I didn't have to use it anymore but gave me a little one if I got sore."

She looked shocked and impressed at the same time. "He did, wow."

"Yeah, I uh," this was the part I was dreading. There was no way of knowing if she'd be cool with my magic or not. "I used my magic to heal my shoulder. Not completely. I still lack some strength, and parts of my arm are still numb. I get shooting pains every so often, so clearly, I'm not a hundred percent, but my surgeon said I was much farther along than he expected."

Her eyes slowly looked back up at me, and her fingers stopped typing. "Magic? Did you go see someone?"

I shook my head. "No, my own magic. I'm a witch."

"Oh!" She smiled and went back to typing. "Okay, well, that makes sense." I felt relieved. She seemed like she'd be cool with the magic stuff. "I've never actually met anyone who has done that." She looked over at me. "Maybe you could show me what you did, and then we can include your magic in your recovery?" I couldn't help but laugh. I had never heard anyone being so positive about my magic before.

"Yeah, that sounds amazing." Avis was great, she wasn't afraid of my magic, and for an hour, we worked in tandem as I played with thick slime to get the strength back in my fingers. I stood next to the wall, my right arm against it, and pushed. I was surprised at how hard it all was.. After an hour, I was exhausted.

"Good work today. I think with your magic and what we do physically will really speed your recovery. Your paperwork says twice a week, so why don't you head to the desk and get your sessions scheduled for the next four weeks, and we'll do an assessment then."

"Sounds great, I'm glad you're not put off by my magic."

She shook her head with a smile. "Oh, not at all. This'll be a great learning experience for both of us."

"I agree. See you later."

"Have a good day." She started typing on her laptop, and I walked back to the desk.

Richard walked over to me and put a hand on my back. "How ya feeling?"

I sighed and laid my head on the front desk. "I am exhausted, and I hurt."

The secretary smiled and started typing. "Ice will help with that. So, when are we thinking?" I put in for the next seven appointments, and I made sure they were towards the end of the day because if today was any indication of how I'd feel afterwards, I didn't feel like having to spend hours at work afterwards. I would be useless with a capital U.

We got in Richard's car, and I used my left arm to buckle my seatbelt. "Do I have to go back to work?"

He chuckled and kissed my forehead. "Yeah, but you can just sit at your desk. Maybe Gwen will be around, and you can talk to her about Olin."

I sighed. "I can do that, but I cannot cook tonight."

"Don't worry, Sweetheart, I got you."

———

Twenty minutes later, we walked into the precinct and sat at our desks. I turned to Gwen, stifling a yawn.

"So, did you find anything out about Olin or that spell?"

"I did!" I smiled at her enthusiasm. She pulled out a little book and turned to me. Her smile disappeared in an instant. "Fuck, you look exhausted. Are you okay?"

I waved her off. "First physical therapy. I am worn out."

"Ooh, sorry," her face scrunched up in sympathy. "You up for this?"

I nodded and moved a book I had on my desk. "Yeah, I'm good, what do you got?"

She scooted over and opened the book, putting it where I cleared some space. "Okay, so let's start with Olin. He owns a landscaping business in Woodhurst, and the poor guy lost his wife six months ago in a house fire. They are both shifters, wolf, and she, uh," she took a deep breath. "She was pregnant."

My shoulders lowered at the realization. "Fuck."

"Shit, really?" Richard turned to us. "He must be in agony over that alone."

Gwen nodded. "Yeah. And a few months after that, his brother was killed in a car wreck. He was T-boned by a drunk driver. She's in custody awaiting arraignment currently."

This poor guy. "What was his brother's name?"

"Dimitri."

Hyde came over and leaned on my desk. "Talking about the brother?" He put his thumbs in the straps of his vest.

"Yeah." Gwen turned and looked up at her new partner.

"Did he have a girlfriend?" Richard scooted closer to the three of us.

"I didn't see anything in the report," Hyde said. "But if we end up talking to Olin about it, we can ask him. I'm sure he'd know."

I nodded, fighting my eyelids. "Yeah, probably."

"Man, you look worn out, Roa," Hyde said with a smile.

"Had therapy today. I got to play with slime."

Richard snickered behind me while Hyde gave a whistle. "Ooh, playtime, that's rough," he teased.

"You'd be surprised."

Gwen gave his vest a little smack, and he chuckled. "Okay, so that spell," Gwen slid in her chair back over to her desk and got another book, then slid back. "I think this is it." She opened it to a page she had marked with a velvet bookmark and sat it on the desk. "It requires the one with the bond to have a broken heart. Anyone can do the spell, so it's not exclusively fae in nature, which I think is lucky." I nodded in agreement. It sure sounded like the spell in question.

"How so?" Hyde asked, leaning on my desk.

"If it were a fae spell, we'd have a harder time finding it and most likely wouldn't be able to break it either. Unless we find a fae to do it for us," I explained.

Gwen nodded in agreement and went back to the book. "So, if it is this one, the fae will know we're trying to break it and could act through him. They won't know we're talking about it, thankfully, and won't know until we start. So, if he agrees to it, we'll have to tie him down or something."

"He's a shifter, right?" Richard spoke up, and we all turned to him. "He'll probably already have something for that."

"True," I sighed. "If not, I'm sure someone will let him use theirs." I gave Richard's foot a little kick. "Tomorrow, we'll find Olin and see if he'll talk to us. It might help that we met him yesterday."

"You met him already?" Hyde shifted on his feet, and my eyes went wide.

Shit. Thankfully Richard was a fast thinker. "Mabon introduced us. You know the guy who owns Jolly Bear Barista?"

Hyde nodded. "Oh right, good drinks. Guess shifters hang together."

"Yep." I had to remember to thank Richard for that later. "If he agrees to this, I'll let you know. It can't hurt to have some backup with this."

"I'll await your signal." Gwen slid back to her desk, and Hyde joined her.

I turned back to Richard and grimaced. "Almost boned that one."

He chuckled. "I got you."

———

That night, I was glad to be home. I was super sore even

hours later. So sore, I gave in and put my arm in the little sling while we were still at the precinct and grumbled when it felt better. When we got to my apartment, Richard walked straight to the kitchen and started making dinner for us, and I once again was grateful for him. I popped some ibuprofen and went into my witchy room for some books.

"Whatcha got that on for Hen?" I turned and saw Will standing at the doorway to the room. Not entering like I asked him not to, and I instantly remembered what was burning a hole in my pocket.

"First physical therapy today. It was rough, so letting my arm rest."

"Hello, Will," Richard called out from the kitchen when he heard me talking.

"Evening Detective."

"He said, 'Evening Detective'." I pulled a book out and walked it back to the couch.

"How are you liking your new home?" I smiled that Richard was talking to Will. I didn't think he talked to many people who couldn't hear him.

"It's grand, thank you for asking. Peaceful and safe, but I wish she were home more so I could see her bonny face." He leaned close to me and pinched my cheeks as he said that.

I swatted him away, and he laughed as he floated another book over to me. "He said, 'It's grand. Thank you for asking.'"

Richard laughed. "Why'd you swat at him?"

I shook my head and opened a book. "He was pinching my cheeks."

He snickered. "Why?"

I sighed. "He said he wished I were home more so he could see my bonny face." I heard his chuckle float in from the kitchen.

"What does bonny mean?" I watched Will sit next to me. He leaned back and wiggled his eyebrows.

I rolled my eyes at him. "It means beautiful."

"Ooh," he teased. "Well, he's right, you are beautiful."

I turned and smiled at him. "Thank you." Will was snickering next to me and put another book on the table for me. "And thank you. Will?"

He leaned back against the couch, his arms crossed. "Hmm?"

"I…found out more about your past, if you're interested?"

His eyes roamed over me for a moment. "What was it?"

"Your children."

His eyes went wide. "My bairns?" He nodded and scooted closer. "Tell me, Hen." I pulled out the paper and laid it on the table so he could read it. He leaned over the paper, and I could hear him whispering as he read. He put his hand on his chest and sat back. "My bairns," he smiled. "My sweet…I had five bairns, Hen."

I smiled and wiped away a tear. "You did. I feel sorry for your wife."

He laughed and looked at the paper again. "She wanted every single one. Oh, little Arabella," he ran his finger over her name. "We named her after my sister. She died when she was a wee thing, my sister, not my daughter," he quickly said.

I smiled. "Gotcha."

"Thomas was the only one born in America. The rest were born in Scotland. My whole family came with us. All my brothers and their wives, my parents. We were going to start a whole new life here."

"Did you?"

He nodded. "For a while, it was heaven on Earth." He

picked up the paper and disappeared, taking the paper with him to wherever ghosts take things.

"How'd he take it?" Richard called out from the kitchen.

I turned and laid my arm on the back of the couch. "Better than I thought he would."

"Good." I started rifling through the books while Richard stirred something in a metal bowl. "So, what are you looking for?"

I flipped through yet another book that wasn't being helpful. "Bonding spells and how to get rid of them."

"Do you think Olin knows he has one in him?"

"I honestly have no idea. But a lot of these kinds of spells are put on people without their knowledge. He could be doing this fae's dirty work and not even be aware of it."

The stirring noise stopped. "Shit."

"Yeah." I sniffed, and my nose couldn't quite figure out what it smelled, and I half wondered if Will was pranking me. It smelled good, but there was a stinky aspect to it as well. "Why does it smell like farts?"

Richard laughed. "I'm making egg salad sandwiches. You're running low on food, so that's what I came up with."

"Yeah, I should put in an order." Since grocery shopping was difficult with one arm, I started ordering them and getting them delivered. I kinda liked not having to spend an hour and a half in a grocery store over the months.

"You should go shopping. It might be good for your shoulder." I smiled and realized that I could go shopping again. I could walk around listening to music with my chai like a regular person. But after my arm stopped hurting.

"You're so smart." He walked over and set down two plates with egg salad sandwiches and potato chips.

"So are you." I sat my book down and moved the others out of the way so I wouldn't spill food on them.

"Thank you." I leaned over, and he gave me a kiss.

"You're welcome, Sweetheart." I picked up the sandwich, and it was pretty tasty. Admittedly, I hadn't eaten many egg salad sandwiches over the years, but maybe I should have been. It was tangy and eggy. Maybe he just knew how to make good ones. "So, besides the spell, do you think Olin is our guy?" He used a big potato chip to scoop up some egg bits that had fallen out of his sandwich.

I swallowed my bite and brushed some crumbs off my hands. "I saw the creature that supposedly enthralled Glass. The size of it really got my attention. When Olin introduced himself, I couldn't help but notice the similarities. With that bond in him, I'd say he's as close to a suspect as we're going to find."

"Jeez, poor guy, this is the last thing he needs." He took a bite of his sandwich. "Are the culprits always glowy when you cast that spell?" I sat back and thought about what I knew and what I had seen over the years. When I did see them, they weren't glowy, not like that. I remembered a case a few years ago where a fae had enthralled a human. They stood in the room with their shining victim, but the fae was normal, and while shiny, I could still see the human perfectly.

"No, they're not."

"You think it was a way to hide him from your spell or something?" I remembered the Sluagh that killed Howard and his wife. It was purposely hiding from me in a way where I saw absolutely nothing. No shadow, no footsteps, just nothing. I took another bite of my sandwich and thought for a moment. That spell saw the past and what magic was active at the time. And the person in the corner was glowing, like I had seen Glass glow in the interrogation room, more so even. Making someone so glowy I couldn't see them would be a sneaky way to hide someone's identity.

"Mother fuc—" Richard's phone rang. "Are you serious?"

He chuckled and answered his phone, "Moss." I couldn't hear the other side of the conversation this time. "Damn, okay, I'll let her know." He hung up and looked over at me.

"Don't tell me there's another one."

"Yep, it's fresh, though. The body is still at the scene. Hyde and Gwen are there, and he figured it might be good if we were there too since it was her first crime scene." That spike of adrenaline hit me like it always did before a scene. It helped push back my exhaustion, but I wondered for how long.

"Not a bad idea. All right, let's go. I'll see if the same large, glowy person is there." He nodded and gave my forehead a kiss and packed the food away while I got my special rock and tucked it into my pocket. "Don't mess with our sandwiches, Will!"

"No promises, my bonny Hen!" I heard before the door shut.

———

When we got to the scene, it was indeed still active. The lights of the emergency vehicles were lighting the night as neighbors stood on their porches to see what was going on. We walked inside after putting on gloves and booties. Hyde and Gwen met us in the living room before we saw anything. She looked a little more subdued but not horrified. I took that as a good sign.

"First murder scene?" I asked as we stopped in front of them.

"Yeah, not first body, though. How you feeling? I told Hyde we didn't need to call you since you were so tired."

"Oh, I'm fine. Adrenaline is a hell of a thing." And it was true. I wasn't as worn out, but I knew it'd hit me like a brick to the face later.

Hyde nudged her with his elbow. "See? I told you she'd be fine."

Moss looked over at Hyde. "What do we have?" Hyde cleared his throat and motioned back to the scene, which was in a kitchen.

"This one is a bit different than the others. The suspect called 911 and said they killed their girlfriend, and then they killed themselves."

My eyes went wide. "What?"

"Yeah, it was too late by the time anyone got here. The suspect stabbed their girlfriend and then used the same knife on their throat. It's messy in there."

I felt Richard's hand on my shoulder. "I'm going to do my spell." He nodded and took a step back. "Gwen, put your hand on my shoulder. You should be able to see what I do." She nodded and did just that as I put my palms together and cast my spell. It spread through the house, and I saw two women in the kitchen making dinner.

"Gosh, they look happy," Gwen's voice was quiet as she watched. They did look happy, moving about the kitchen, making salad, and pouring wine. They smiled at each other and kissed several times. Then one of them, she had short brown hair, stopped and looked into the living room. I turned and saw the same large, glowy figure pointing at her, and I had no doubt in my mind that it was Olin. Same height, shoulder width, and even smelled the same. I shoved my hand into my pocket and felt it buzzing in my hand. There was fae magic here, no doubt.

"What do you see, Gwen? What do you smell?"

I heard her sniff. "Dirt, and musk, smells like a wolf-shifter, all right." I was impressed at that. "I see something huge, but I can't tell what it is."

"See anything, Roa?" I heard Hyde ask.

"I do," I turned to him as the woman with the short hair shoved a kitchen knife in her throat. "But it's not good."

"Why was the suspect all glowy?" Gwen took her hand off my shoulder. "We should be able to see them with the spell."

"That's the insane bit. I assume the fae put a spell on him to keep his identity hidden. Wouldn't do them any good if we knew who he was and arrested him." Gwen crossed her arms and held her chin. I noticed how she was staring at the place the large suspect once was instead of the crime scene.

"It really does seem like they're enthralled, doesn't it?"

"Yeah." Gwen and I looked at each other, and I knew I looked just as worried as she did. If someone was enthralling others to kill, we had a whole new problem on our hands. I looked over at Richard. He was across the living room looking at a group of pictures on the wall. "What do you see?" He picked up a frame off the wall and walked back over to me.

"Look." He held out the frame, and I saw a picture of the couple, smiling and holding a little trophy with an axe on it. Next to it was a certificate for first place at an axe throwing tournament at Solstice Axe Throwing.

"Oh shit."

———

An hour later, Richard and I were in the morgue with Nicola, and the new M.E., Dr. Laurette Terraiu, was there as well. She was shorter than Nicola but, again, taller than me. She wore dark-rimmed glasses, and her dark hair was pulled back into a ponytail. She was from France, so listening to her talk was fascinating. At the moment, she was just shadowing Nicola to get the hang of things. The two victims were on morgue tables side-by-side, a cloth pulled up to their necks. I swore I could still see tear marks down their faces.

"So, the suspect killed the victim, then herself?" Nicola looked up at us, and we nodded. "That's different from the others."

"Yeah, I'm not sure why she was able to overcome the compulsion. From what I saw, the suspect didn't tell her to kill herself, so I'll have to do more reading on that spell. I did see the suspect point to her phone on the table. I assumed to call 911 and confess, which she did. But then she just…killed herself."

She blew a low whistle and shook her head. "Any idea what the suspect might be?"

"I have one idea. But I think it's being controlled by a fae, which makes things even more tricky."

"Why's that?" Laurette asked as she kept studying the bodies.

"It can be hard to prove it's fae and not the creature, so we'd have to find either the suspect or the fae casting the spell on them. And then prove they aren't working in tandem."

"Huh, that does sound convoluted." Laurette walked around the bodies. "Any way to prove it?"

I sighed and crossed my arms. "Yeah, I think so." I looked over at Richard. He was studying the bodies, his hands on his hips. "Feel like taking a walk?"

He looked and nodded. "Whatever you need."

I held my hand out to Dr. Terraiu. "Nice to meet you, I hope you like Arion."

"Nice to meet you as well." She shook hands with Richard, and we left the two smart women to do what smart women do.

———

The sliver of moon wasn't giving us much light as we walked into the woods just outside of town. Thankfully, Richard had a few little LED flashlights in his car. They worked really well for being so small.

He moved a large branch out of my way, but I still ducked as I walked past. "So, what are we doing?"

"I think it's time to see if any fae will talk to me." I stopped at a huge oak tree. "Keep an ear out. Sometimes other things can be attracted by the summoning." He nodded and started scanning the woods around us. So far, there were the usual noises, owls, wind blowing leaves, no growling, which was always good. I laid my hand on the trunk of the tree and closed my eyes. "Great fae of the forest, I beg you, grant me an audience. I fear someone is trying to blame fae for horrid crimes in the human world. I want to make sure the one responsible is brought to justice. I need your help, please." I pushed my power into the tree, and I felt the life it held. It was old, strong, and warm. I felt my magic spread from the tree into the forest, and I took my hand off it.

Richard turned to me. "Now what?"

"We wait."

An hour later, we were sitting against the tree, watching a mouse skitter through the leaves around us. I knew it might take a while to see if anyone answered, and it could be a big If. Fae never did anything they didn't want to, and answering to humans was at the bottom of their list.

"So, I take it the last time we encountered a fae, it was rare?" Richard stretched his legs out in front of him.

"Yeah. The chief wanted to know what happened to his daughter, otherwise he wouldn't have bothered. And now that he knows, he has no obligation to come this time." I laced my fingers with Richard's and squeezed his hand. "Not that I'd expect *him* to come, he's the chief, he's too busy for something like this."

"I get that." He raised my hand and gave it a kiss. "Will they just show up wherever, or does it have to be here?"

"Right now, it'll be here. We'll give it another hour, then I'll just keep an eye out for a little bauble we can use to summon them directly, like that acorn he gave us."

"Gotcha." He leaned over and kissed my head. I looked up at him, and he kissed my lips. "Do fae often make other creatures do their dirty work?" My skin prickled with energy as the leaves in front of us were lifted in the air by unseen hands.

"No, we don't." A soft, annoyed voice made my ears twitch as the leaves settled, and we saw a female fae standing before us. We quickly got to our feet. No need to annoy her more by being rude. She was as tall as I was, with light green skin, and was wearing a dress of dried daisies. Her dark hair was in multiple braids down the back of her head.

"Thank you for coming," I said. "My name is —"

"I know who you are. You are The Witch of Arion, and that is your mate. You helped the chief find his youngest daughter's killer."

Yikes, I had no idea our reputation preceded us like that. "We did, yes."

She looked between us. "And you call on us again?"

"Technically, he called us the first time, but yeah. There have been several murders in town, and I think a fae might be making someone else commit them."

She walked around us, sniffing the air. "What makes you say it's fae?" I pulled out my special rock and held it out to her. It was buzzing like crazy in my hand from being so close to her.

"This detects fae magics, and it reacted at the scene of the crimes." Her hand hovered over the rock, and I knew she'd be able to tell I was being truthful.

"Then a fae was responsible for the murders?"

"That's what we're unsure of," Richard spoke up. "It seems the one telling the humans to kill their loves is themselves under a fae compulsion as well."

Her head snapped up at that. "Killing their loves?"

"Yes. One woman ended up killing herself after she killed her girlfriend, but the first man called the authorities and admitted he did it. When I broke the compulsion, he didn't remember what he had done at first. Then we showed him pictures from the crime scene, and he remembered."

The fae woman looked down and held her chin as she thought. "Tell me more." I told her everything I could remember, to seeing a huge shape at the crime scene to why I believed they were under the compulsion. Even how Glass was going to propose to his girlfriend and how distraught he was when learning what he had done. She paced while I talked, and Richard put a hand on my back.

Finally, she stopped and looked at us. "I feel you are correct in your assumptions that a fae is making another creature do these things." I could hear the disappointment in her voice and hoped that meant she'd be able to help.

"Might you have something that could aid us in figuring out who either one is before more people are killed?" It could be dangerous requesting something like this from fae, but I hoped that since she looked worried about what was going on, it meant she would actually give a shit.

Her head snapped up to ours. "Perhaps." She waved her hand and disappeared.

Richard took a step forward and looked around. "Where

did she go?"

"To look, I assume. I hope." I took his hand and started for the car. "They do things on their own time, but maybe since this will give fae a bad name, she'll work a little faster."

He put an arm around my waist as we walked. "I hope so. Back to the books?" All I really wanted to do was sleep. The adrenaline had long worn off.

"Maybe for a bit, but I'm tired, and I'm hungry."

He kissed my forehead. "Thank goodness we still have dinner waiting for us."

"Do uh…do you think we're needed anymore?"

He wrapped his arms around me. "Hyde called me for more as a consultant for Gwen, so they can be on point for this one. So, I don't think so."

I smiled. "Good." My stomach growled. "Let's finish dinner."

"Deal."

———

We walked into my apartment, and I threw my purse onto the couch and walked to the fridge.

"Really should have finished dinner before we left." I pulled my sandwich out of the fridge and opened the container it was in. It was still just as good cold as it was warm. "Who knew something that smelled like farts could taste so good." Richard laughed and leaned against the counter, watching me eat. "Aren't you gonna eat?" I swallowed my last bite and quickly drank some water. I doubted he wanted my breath to smell like eggs at the moment.

"I will, don't worry." He picked me up like a princess and carried me to my room. "But you need to rest. After therapy and all that magic and hiking, you have to be exhausted. No books either."

I kind of liked this pushy side of him. "Wasn't much of a hike."

He snickered. "You need to rest." He tossed me on the bed, and I laughed. "You can do research tomorrow. I'll clean up and join you in a moment."

"Okay." He walked back to the kitchen, and I kicked my shoes off when I noticed Will standing by the doorframe. He was staring at the bed, his arms crossed over his chest. "You all right?" His eyes turned to me, and he nodded before he went invisible. "Okay," I whispered and pulled a large t-shirt out of my dresser and went into the bathroom. Even with the sandwich in my stomach, I could feel the day catching up with me. Another murder, another couple torn apart for no reason. It was heartbreaking.

CHAPTER 7

I felt much better the next morning. Food and sleep were clearly what I needed after therapy. Richard made us waffles, and we scarfed them down before leaving for work. I had a few books in a backpack that I figured I could peruse for how to break a compulsion spell. One of them belonged to the Fells, and I was going to start with that one. They always had the perfect books.

We walked to our desks and saw an acorn laying in the middle of mine. "Perfect," I picked it up. "Moss wanna come with me?" Richard turned, and I opened my hand to show him.

"Yeah, where to?"

"Not far." He followed me, and we walked across the street to the little park in the middle of town. He pulled out his trusty little notebook, and I threw the acorn on the ground, breaking it open. A nearby tree creaked and groaned as we watched a portal open, and the same fae from the night before crawled through and stood before us.

"Thank you for coming." I gave her a little nod as she stood next to the tree and looked around.

"This is the town?" I could see a hint of distaste on her face.

"Yes. This is Arion."

"I've never seen it." She sniffed the air. "Small."

I nodded. "It is." I didn't dare ask her what she found. She'd tell me when she was ready, and if I pissed her off, she'd keep it to herself.

"I don't understand how Thicket could stand it." I jumped a little at the mention of Howard's elven wife.

"Honestly, I don't know how much of the town she saw. No one knew she was married to Howard." She turned back to us, and I could have sworn I saw a hint of sadness in her eyes.

"That's right, I had forgotten."

"Did you know Thicket?" It was probably a stupid question. She was one of the Chief's daughters. I imagine it was the same in the fae realm as it was here. The family of those in charge were usually known by many.

She held her chin, and it looked like she was trying to decide what to tell us. "Thicket was the youngest of us."

"In your realm?" I felt Richard's hand on my back as he asked that.

"Of my sisters." Oh shit.

"I'm sorry for your loss." And I meant it, of course, but it felt like it was too little too late.

"Thank you. So, your intuition was correct." Right to it then, I liked that. "The creature is being manipulated by a fae." I wasn't sure Olin would like being referred to as a creature, but I wasn't going to let anyone else know what I thought until after I got rid of that spell. I didn't trust the fae to find him first and do something to him that would keep him out of our hands.

"I went by the scenes and could feel familiar magic and the energy of a shifter."

"The magic was familiar?" I heard Richard's pen flying across the paper behind me.

She looked past me at him, and I could tell she was sniffing the air. "I have felt that magic before. It is from a fae called Eldora, and she spends a great deal of time alone. I was able to sense it was her magic creating the compulsions."

"What makes her magic different from someone else's?" Richard coming in clutch with the important questions.

"Every fae's magic is unique to them. Eldora's magic is the saddest magic I've ever encountered. I fear her magic has turned dark." Hearing this fae's magic was sad made me wonder if that was the reason I'd had such a tough time getting these crime scenes out of my mind. Her emotions were rubbing off on me.

"Why is her magic sad?" I noticed a man riding a bicycle past, staring at us, a not so friendly look on his face, so I motioned for him to turn around. He grumbled and peddled away faster.

The fae crossed her arms over her stomach. "She has lost a great deal over her long life and is constantly searching for ways to fill that empty space in her heart." That didn't make much sense to me, but I wasn't an ageless fae with eons of heartbreak under my belt, either.

"If she was sad about losing people, why would she make others lose them as well?"

She shifted quietly on her feet. "Like I said, I fear her magic has turned dark. She may want others to feel as she does but doesn't want to get blood on her hands in a literal sense. So, she found someone else who might feel the same as her."Her eyes met mine. "Do you have any suspects?" The way she asked it, I knew she had an idea about who this Eldora had bound to her. She had a little sass that if you didn't speak with fae much, you might miss it.

"We have our suspicions, yes." Never be a know-it-all in front of fae. They take offense sometimes.

"What I could tell about the shifter is they are male, but I already checked the one male wolf shifter in town, and he is not under, nor has ever been under a fae compulsion. I don't have time to check the surrounding areas."

I nodded. "That's the conclusion we came to as well, and don't worry, we'll get right on it."

"Look for a shifter who is alone, male, and has lost a lot. He could be your victim." Every step we took in this matter made it seem more like Olin, which was good and bad. Good because we knew where to find him. Bad because, well, he was bonded to a fae against his will.

"Technically, he's a suspect," Richard said, still writing.

"Technically, he's a victim as well, as it is clear he didn't want to do this." I could hear her getting annoyed, so I quickly stepped in front of him.

"Because if he did want to do these things, she wouldn't have compelled him."

She nodded. "Exactly."

"Would you happen to know where we can find this Eldora? I take it if I summoned her, she wouldn't answer." She shook her head and squinted at a small child across the park that was staring at her.

"No, she would not." I noticed she waved her hand, and a pretty red flower popped up in front of the child. I heard their tiny gasp from where we were standing and fought hard not to smile. "I looked around but found no trace of her. So, I let guards know she is causing trouble. No one has been able to find her yet. If we find her first, I will let you know, and *we* will take care of her."

"As long as you can give us proof it was her, we won't try and drag her in," Richard said.

She gave him a curt nod. "Easily done. Is that all?"

"Yes, thank you for everything. You've been a tremendous help." She stepped back into the tree without a word, and we watched it close. The sounds of birds made my ears twitch. I didn't even realize how quiet it had gotten.

"Well," I turned, my arms crossed over my stomach. "Wolf, sad, dude. Sure, does seem like Olin."

He put the notebook in his back pocket. "Did you still want to talk to him today?"

"Yes, we need to hurry before she makes him do something else." We walked back into the precinct, and I saw Gwen at her desk. "Hey, Gwen, can I have that folder you have on Olin?"

"Sure." She pulled it out of her drawer and handed it to me.

"Thanks, and can you and Hyde check to see if Glass or his girlfriend had gone to that axe-throwing place in Woodhurst as well?"

"Can do, got a hunch?"

"Yep." I put the folder in my backpack, and we jumped into Richard's car and headed to Woodhurst.

————

As Richard drove, I read what Gwen found about Olin York. He owned a landscaping business like she said. He was thirty-two years old and grew up in Woodhurst and was born a shifter like his wife. They had been married five years when the fire happened. He wasn't home and made a big stink about how she should have gotten out. I had to agree with him. With her being a shifter, she could have smelled the fire a lot earlier than a human would have. Maybe I'd have Nicola pull up her autopsy report. Not that I wanted to open another can of worms, but you never know, so I pulled my phone out and gave her a little text about it.

"What do you have on Olin's brother?" Richard asked as he drove.

My eyes scanned the pages for a moment. "His name was Dimitri. He worked with his brother on the landscaping business. The accident happened two months after his wife died like Mabon said." I grimaced at that. "The wreck happened around eleven at night, and he was t-boned at the intersection of Franklin and Dahlia." Those names rang a bell. "I think I remember that it was bad."

Richard nodded. "The suspect was drunk and texting her boyfriend at the time."

"Hmm. Well, it is a lot of tragedy, and the shape of him matches, and then there's that spell I felt on him. But doesn't it still seem kinda random?"

He nodded. "It does. But that fae said Eldora was getting dark, so it could be anything. Hell, he could look like an old lover or something." I put the folder away and pulled out one of my books and turned it to the bonding spell page when I realized my faux pas.

"Oh, shit, I never did ask the fae her name, did I?" I sighed and turned back to my book. "Crap, oh well."

Richard chuckled. "I'm sure if she took it as an insult, she would have thrown it at us at some point."

"Probably. I can't believe she's Thicket's sister. I wonder if that's why she came, she felt she owed us something for finding the Sluagh."

Richard shrugged. "Could be. I don't know much about fae. Maybe they were close once?"

"Maybe." My fingers skimmed the words, and I found what I was looking for and mentally thanked Jackson and Amelia. "Okay, I think I can break that spell on him, but he's not gonna like it."

"Didn't think he would."

Olin's business was so profitable he had his own building he worked out of, and the address was in the file, so we drove there first. Like expected, it was well maintained, with lots of flowers and pretty bushes around a well-manicured lawn. Thankfully, there was a big red truck in the parking lot, I hoped that it was his. We parked near the truck and walked inside. It was nice and cool and smelled like pine.

"Be right there!" We heard him from the back.

"You know, this really seems like the type of conversation you have over Chinese or something. Not at work." Richard chuckled and rubbed my back as Olin walked in from wherever he was earlier.

When he saw us, his eyes lit up. "Hey, Richard and Lily, right? From the other night?" He walked over and shook our hands.

"That's us," Richard said. "How are you?"

"Oh, fine. You need some yard work done?" He clapped his hands together once, looking like he was excited about making some money.

"No, not at the moment. Actually, can we sit somewhere private?" I let Richard take the lead on this bit. I had a hard enough job trying to explain to him that I thought he was unwillingly bound to a fae. At least, I hope it was unwilling.

"You, uh, got something on my wife or brother's case?" His voice was quiet but strong. I had to admire him for that.

"Not exactly. It's hard to explain."

He looked between us for a moment. "All right." He nodded, and we followed him back to the office, and we all sat on a couch across from his desk.

I laid my hands in my lap and steeled myself. "So, as you know, Richard is a detective in Arion, while I am a magical consultant."

Realization gleamed in his eyes. "Oh, you're that witch they have, aren't you?"

"I am." At least he didn't sneer when he said it.

"We have some on our force, but I think they're treated better. I heard rumors that Arion didn't really appreciate their witches."

I chuckled. "I think it's getting better."

"Good," he looked like he realized something. "Wait a sec, you guys are dating." He pointed at us, a sneaky smile on his face. "Is that allowed?"

My eyes went wide, duh, he saw us kiss and hug at the axe throwing place. "Oh, uh, yes, we are."

Richard sat forward a bit. "We aren't exactly sure how it's supposed to work."

"Maybe keep that to yourself?" I gave him a hopeful smile.

He chuckled. "Will do. So, what did you have to tell me?"

I sighed and sat up straight. "We have been looking into some murders in town, and while I know you are not responsible," I made sure he understood that we didn't think he was a suspect. "I think you might be an unwilling accomplice," I said gently.

His eyes went wide as he looked between us. "I haven't killed anyone!" I could feel his power start rippling out from him, and my arms broke out in goosebumps.

Richard raised a hand. "We know, but Miss Roa has a suspicion that you might be under a compulsion of sorts from a fae."

"The fuck?" He turned to me. "I have been through enough in the last six months. I don't need this shit too!" I understood his anger, hell I was angry for him, but I hoped we could keep him calm enough to explain before he stormed off or wolfed out or whatever it is they do.

"I agree, which is why I want to try and get that spell off of you. We're still trying to figure out if there's some connection between you and the fae who put it on you. Because it just seems too random to us."

He sat back, crossing his arms. "I don't know any fae." He rubbed his face, and I could see he was fighting tears. Nothing worse than crying in front of people you don't know. "Personally, at least."

I glanced up at Richard a moment. "Personally?"

He sniffed and lowered his head. "My brother was dating a fae when he was killed. I never met her, but he said he loved her. She didn't show up at the funeral. I had hoped to meet her then, but no." My witchy senses were tingling at that, or it was my feminine instincts. They went hand in hand sometimes.

"Do you know her name?"

He nodded at me. "Eldora." Richard's eyes snapped to mine. "That mean something?"

"I think we have our link." Richard nodded, and I turned back to Olin. "We learned the name of the fae who put this spell on you is Eldora. The fae we spoke to told us that Eldora's magic had gotten dark recently. That she had experienced a lot of heartache in her long life."

He was quiet for a moment, contemplating what I had just told him. "You think when my brother was killed, it sent her over the edge or something?"

"It's a possibility." Richard nodded.

He nodded and sat forward, staring down at his open hands. "You sure I have something in me? I don't feel any different."

"I don't think you would. It makes it easier to control you.

But do you have any moments of lost time or things you can't explain lately?" The way he wouldn't meet my eyes, I knew he had. "Let me see what I can do. First, do you have any manacles or something around here? She could tell I'm trying to get it out of you, and it could get messy."

"Really?" He looked up as we both nodded. He ran a hand through his hair and licked his lips. "If that's the case, why don't we do this with the help of my pack. I can get everyone together tonight. We'll gather in my basement. I have manacles, and they can help if…something happens."

"That's a good idea." I patted his hand. "Maybe we'll bring our other witch and her partner too."

He got to his feet. "The more the merrier." He sighed and put his hands in his pockets. "Are you sure she won't know what we're trying to do?"

"I don't believe so, not until I actually start to get rid of the spell."

He nodded. "Okay." He started to turn but stopped. "You don't think she'd make me do something until then, do you?"

I shrugged. "Honestly, I have no idea. But all the murders happened at night, so if she keeps to that schedule, you should be fine."

"Yeah, makes sense." Poor guy sounded so sad. "I can give you my address if you need it."

Richard took out his phone. "That'd be great, thanks." He typed the address in his phone. It was the same as where the fire was, so I assumed he had fixed the fire damage. We shook his hand and told him we'd see him later, then walked back to Richard's car.

"I hope the pack can help," he said as he shut the door.

"I think they will. Not only will we have some more

backup, but I think it'll help him when it's out of him. Who knows how he'll be emotionally? He's already fragile." I laid my hand on my chest. I could practically feel his heartache out here.

"True." I texted Gwen and Hyde to meet us at Olin's house at seven that night and that his pack was going to help us support him while we got that bond out of him. I got a big green thumbs up from Gwen and a 'You got it' from Hyde. I didn't know how many shifters there were in Woodhurst, so hopefully, his basement had enough room.

———

At seven, we both pulled up to Olin's house. There were already half a dozen cars parked in the driveway and in the street.

"Got his little present?" I could hear Richard teasing me about the necklace I put a spell on for Olin.

I reached into my pocket and patted the little necklace. "Like I could forget it." We got out, and Gwen walked over to us, her arms hugging herself.

"Lot of people here."

"Yeah. I think it's going to be a good thing." I laced my arm through hers and led the way to the door. "I've never done magic around a pack before."

"Me neither," she leaned closer. "You think any of them are gonna be cute?"

I snickered and rang the doorbell. "Probably." The door opened, and a tall man I didn't recognize was standing there. He had to be over six feet, and his dark hair was in a long ponytail behind his head. He looked to be in his early thirties, and his arms were so muscular I had to concentrate not to stare at them. His smile instantly calmed me, I could practically feel his power while he was just standing there doing nothing. It was impressive. This guy had to be high up in the pack.

"Lily?" His voice was deep and soothing.

"That's me." I gave a little wave. "This is Gwen, Officer Hyde, and Detective Moss."

"Nice to meet you, I'm Luan, pack alpha." Ah, an alpha, yep made sense. We walked in and shook hands with him as we passed. He had an amazing handshake, perfect pressure, and friendly. The house was full of people, and I couldn't help but feel a little jealous. "Thank you so much for helping Olin with this," Luan said. "He's been through too much lately. Hopefully, you can find this Eldora and give our boy some peace."

"It's absolutely no trouble. No one deserves this, least of all him." I looked around at all the people, just going about their business, it seemed. "I'm glad so many of you showed up. I think it'll help him after this is all done."

Luan smiled. "He's part of our pack. We help everyone when they need it." For some reason, I assumed Olin was going to be the head wolf in charge. I was surprised to learn he wasn't. It was nice to see that they helped, even if he was low on the proverbial totem pole. There were some members in the kitchen making a bunch of food that smelled amazing. There were a few couples in the living room with children. From the tingle of magic in the air, I could tell every person here was a shifter. It felt like family coming to help. It was refreshing until a sudden wave of grief hit me. It had been years since I felt any grief over my family, but I was a pro at hiding it by now.

I looked over and saw Richard and Hyde talking to some of the shifters in the dining room. Gwen was sitting on the floor in the living room as one of the toddlers demanded she read a squishy book. My traitorous eyes got misty, and I looked down at the ground.

"You all right?" Luan laid a hand on my shoulder, and

I felt his magic. It was clear I had never met an alpha of a pack before because his magic felt like a sturdy brick wall that could withstand anything.

"Yeah, just been a while since I've been around such a big family." He gave me a little smile and crossed his arms as he looked into the living room.

"We're lucky in Woodhurst. There's enough of us that we can help others without it being a detriment to our pack." He looked down at me. "Do you have a big family?"

"I did, once. Just about everyone on my dad's side lived with us or near us when I was a kid."

"What about your mom's side?" I shook my head and looked back at Gwen, jiggling the toddler as she read the book, their little giggles filling the air.

"No, they all live just outside San Miguel de Allende. They didn't come with my parents when they immigrated."

"Oh, why not?" I turned to the tall shifter. He genuinely seemed curious.

I shrugged. "No idea." I heard footsteps and saw Olin coming down the stairs.

"Okay, guess it's time." He sounded tired and nervous. I didn't blame him. Gwen, Richard, and Hyde came over, and I introduced him to those he didn't know.

"If you're ready, we're ready."

He nodded and turned to the big guy. "Let's get this show on the road."

Luan nodded and spoke up. "Okay, everyone helping come down to the basement, everyone else stay up here but stay alert." Five big men, a teenager, and one woman, filed through the kitchen and down into the basement. Luan motioned for us to follow, and he brought up the rear with Olin behind me.

The basement was huge and looked as clean as I expected it to, organized and safe. In the middle of the floor were two pairs of manacles bolted to the cement floor. Two because two shifters used to live here. Olin was barefoot in a pair of gray sweats and a loose tank top. Made sense if he shifted, I guess. Wearing clothes you didn't mind getting ruined and all. Everyone waited as he put his wrists in the manacles and sat on the floor. Luan walked up and stood behind him, and the rest of them formed a semicircle so I could get to him.

"What do you need us to do?" Luan patted Olin on the shoulder, and I could tell it helped him calm down a bit. His shoulders relaxed, and his breathing slowed.

"I'm going to try and get that bond out of him. It will take some time, and there's a good chance the fae will realize what I'm doing and make him...stop me. If you can keep him from hurting me or running off, I'll make sure he'll be free of that spell soon." I turned to Gwen. "I was going to have you keep him still, but I think with his pack here, they can hold him down, so I want you to help me with the spell." She nodded. "Lend me your power, and between the two of us, it won't take as long."

"Gotcha."

I turned to Richard and Hyde. "You guys stand there and look pretty." Everyone laughed. I even saw Olin's shoulders jiggle a little as Hyde did his best model pose, complete with pouty lips. "Ready?" Olin looked up and gave me a nod. "Here we go." I kneeled in front of him, but before I could start, the woman with them spoke up.

"Wait one sec," she dashed to the other side of the basement, then came back with a soft chair pad. "Don't need your knees getting banged up on the floor."

I took it and shoved it under my knees. It was much

more comfortable. "Thanks, that was a good idea." I'd be able to concentrate better if my knees weren't barking at me. I took a deep breath and laid my hand on his shoulder as Gwen laid her hand on mine. "I call upon my magic to find this unwanted bond. Help me free this man from the evil it has spawned." I heard Gwen snort behind me, and I cracked a smile. "Never said I was a poet."

"No kidding." I heard Hyde whisper before he grunted. I assume Richard had elbowed him or something. My magic pushed into Olin's mind, and I didn't have to search long before I found the bond. It was like a lead rope weaving in and out of his soul. It was clear Eldora was powerful. I licked my lips. "This is going to hurt, I'm afraid."

He took a deep breath in through his nose. "I can take it." Luan patted his shoulder.

"Not like that. This bond was created from heartache and loss. I need you to think of your wife. How much you loved each other, the happy times. Can you do that?"

I heard his breath shudder out. "I'll try."

"Good, the happier the memory, the easier it'll be for me to break this bond." I closed my eyes and focused on the magic. I could feel it writhing in him, almost hungrily, waiting for Eldora to tell it to do something. I felt Richard standing behind me, and his sturdy presence helped me focus. . I pictured my magic slowly unraveling that lead rope, bit by bit. I could tell when he thought of a happy memory because it was easier to fray. "Good. Keep it up." I heard him take another shaky breath, and the spell started feeling sticky, harder to pull apart. "Keep thinking about her."

"It's hard to think of happy memories," he said quietly.

"Tell me about your first date." Again, Richard coming in clutch with the support.

Olin took a deep breath. "We went swimming at Meadow Lake. I remember she had on the cutest red swimsuit." That sticky feeling was going away, and I tried to work quickly.

"That was a fun day," Luan spoke up. "I could tell she was getting under your skin fast."

Olin chuckled. "I brought hot dogs to cook over the fire, and she matched me dog for dog." The pack chuckled around us, and I ripped a substantial chunk of the spell out of him.

"She helped me make s'mores," the woman said. "She had the bright idea to put crispy bacon in them. I still make them that way." With the pack's help, the spell was coming apart easier than I ever imagined.

"God, those were good." Olin sighed at the memory. "That night, we laid on our towels and watched the stars. It was the first time I really paid them any mind. But she could make anything fun." I took another chunk out, and that was when I felt her. Eldora. Anger pulsed down that bond, and my arms broke out in goosebumps before I took another chunk of the spell out. I opened my eyes, and it seemed the pack felt it too, as they were all on alert, scooting closer to Olin. I could hear low growls coming from them.

Olin was staring at me. His blue eyes had gone yellow. "Olin?" He started breathing hard, his teeth bared at me.

"Olin, calm yourself." I could feel the power Luan had in his voice, and while Olin's eyes went back to blue, he still looked angry, and I swore his teeth were starting to lengthen.

"Olin, tell me when you knew you loved your wife. Tell me something happy."

"No," he growled like an animal, like a shifter about to shift, and the pack put their arms around him. He jerked a bit, but it seemed like a half-hearted attempt to shake them off. "Leave!"

His voice was more animal than man. Fuuuuck.

"Olin, get a hold of yourself now!" I almost wanted to get a hold of myself from the way Luan was speaking. But he wasn't listening to his alpha and kept trying to shake them off. I could feel the anger that Eldora was pushing down the bond get angrier.

"This isn't you, Olin. Remember, we're trying to help you." Richard tried to reach him, but it was no use. I grabbed his arm, desperately trying to finish the spell.

"I don't want help!" He growled and pulled so hard his right hand broke free of the manacle. Everything was happening in slow motion. Before I could even move my hand, I saw his claw heading for my face. Suddenly, a hairy arm grabbed his and pushed Olin to the floor as he thrashed. It took me a second to realize Luan had shifted, but only partly. He was a huge, furry man with a wolf head and sharp claws. It was then I truly understood just how powerful he was because only the most powerful of shifters could hang onto whatever form they wanted. I watched as the pack gathered around Olin, not caring if he clawed or bit them, which he did, but together they held him down.

"Lily, are you okay?" I felt Richard's hand on my back.

"Yeah, I'm good," I turned to Gwen. "Let's get this bitch out of him."

"Right." I laid my hands on his back, and Gwen did the same to me, and I shoved my magic back into him when I felt a wave of exhaustion roll through me. I just wanted to close my eyes and relax in Richard's arms. My arms dropped to my sides, and I felt Richard's hands on my back.

"Lily!" Luan's voice dragged me from the comforting charm, and I sat up. Damn fae was draining me through him! Well, fuck her.

I put my hands back on Olin. "Are there any candles or anything nearby? I need more energy." Everyone looked around, but I didn't see any.

"How's this?" One of the pack reached into his pocket and held up a Zippo and lit it.

I smiled at his ingenuity. "Any more?" One by one, all of them, but Luan pulled out a lighter and lit them. One of them held up their phone with a picture of a burning candle.

"Sorry, I'm too young to smoke," he said sheepishly.

My smile widened as I felt the energy of the little flames around us. "You shouldn't anyway." I breathed in, "Gwen, get the fire."

"On it." She held out her hand, and we watched as the flames grew. "Don't worry, they won't make your lighters explode."

"Now!" She pulled her now-fisted hand to her chest, and the flames all went out. I felt the rush of energy hum through me, and I ripped down the bond, but my magic kept getting stuck. "He needs to think of his wife!"

"Think about your wife on your wedding day!" Richard yelled over the noise of the thrashing shifter. "How beautiful she was, how happy you were, and how much fun you had that day." I felt the bond start to shred easier, and I worked quickly. "How you couldn't wait to start your lives together. Think about the day you asked her to marry you. How happy you were when she said yes!" My magic raced along the bond, ripping it to shreds.

"Remember how amazing it was when the pack got together after the wedding reception!" The woman yelled. "How we all welcomed her with open arms!" Olin gave one more shudder as I ripped down the bond like it was nothing, tearing it to pieces. The end was there, and so was Eldora's anger, but it was nothing compared to the love surrounding him now. With one last push through, her spell was broken, and I quickly put a spell on him that would keep his mind his own for a few hours.

I gasped and stumbled back into Gwen. Both Richard and Hyde were there in a second, Richard's arms around my waist and Hyde helping Gwen. Olin looked up at me, and I could tell his mind was his own. He was calm, and there was an awareness in his eyes that wasn't there before.

"He's okay now," I told them. "The bond is broken." Slowly, his pack moved back, and Luan slowly shifted back into a human, clothes and all. It was impressive.

"You even?" Luan helped him to his knees and had his hand on the back of Olin's neck.

He nodded. "Yeah, I'm all good now." The pack undid the manacle, and one of them picked up the broken one, shaking his head.

"Definitely complaining about this." I smiled as they all helped him to his feet and gave Olin hugs and manly back pats. I noticed all their gashes and bite marks were healed. Lucky assholes.

"I can't believe that was in me." Olin put a hand on his chest. "I could feel her anger. It was...unending."

"Sure seemed that way," I agreed. He stretched his neck a few times and then his back. The pack made sure he was good before going back up the stairs. All but Luan, anyway, he stayed downstairs with us.

"I'm sorry I swiped at you. I tried not to, I haven't felt that out of control since I started shifting."

"It's all right, I knew it wasn't personal." I reached into my pocket and felt the onyx stone was indeed still, and I sighed in relief. I pulled out the necklace I had made for Olin and handed it to him. "I put a spell on you so she won't be able to put that bond back on you again." The necklace had a little yellow duck hanging from the cord, which admittedly was silly, but it was all I had at the time. "This will be a more long-term solution until we find her and bind her magic." He stared at the little duck but didn't take it. "I know it's kinda silly, but it's what I had at the moment."

"It's not that," Luan spoke up. "The nursery they had decorated before…it had little ducks in it."

"Oh shit." I looked at the necklace and wondered if I had time to make another.

"No, it's okay." Olin reached out and took it from me, immediately putting it around his neck. "Thank you for your help." He took a deep breath. "Am I going to jail?"

I looked back at Richard and Hyde. This was more their territory. "I don't think so," Richard said. "You'll be called on to testify at some point, but you technically didn't do anything. Maybe a little breaking and entering, but with Ms. Roa's testimony, I'm confident it'll get thrown out." Which was true. It was easy to prove everything he did wasn't by his own volition.

He nodded. "Okay. I can't thank you enough." He reached out, and I shook his hand.

"Not a problem at all." I looked up at Luan. "Magically, he's fine, but don't be afraid to baby him in other ways."

Olin scoffed with a smile on his face as Luan put an arm around his shoulders. "Oh, don't worry, we got him." The six of us walked back up the stairs and saw everyone else was eating whatever it was they were cooking earlier, spread out around the house as before. One of the other women walked up and gave Olin a bowl of food and dragged him into the kitchen to sit and eat.

"Feel free to call me if he seems odd or disappears, or even if you just have questions." I wrote down my number on the little paper pad by the telephone. "But I don't anticipate any issues."

Luan looked at it a moment, then turned to me. "Thank you again."

"You are most welcome." We all shook his hand. "It was nice meeting you and your pack."

He smiled as he gave me a hearty shake. "They love meeting new people." He looked over at Gwen. "Especially pretty witches."

I chuckled, and Gwen shook his hand enthusiastically. "We'll see you around." Luan walked us to the front door, and when it shut behind us, I was shocked at how quiet it was all of a sudden. "I don't know about you, but I'm starving."

"Leave that to us," Gwen patted Hyde's back. "We'll meet you back at your place?"

"Okay, sure." We climbed in our respective cars and headed back to Arion.

Richard chuckled and shook his head. "That was incredible, Sweetheart. Are you tired?"

I sighed and leaned back in the seat. "A bit, I'd be more tired if Gwen weren't there helping. Or if the pack didn't bring out their lighters." We chuckled at that. "I didn't expect that, but it's good to know it works."

"They really care about him, I think he'll be fine."

"Me too." I squeezed his hand. "I felt grief over my family for the first time in years as I looked at them all."

"I'm sorry," he leaned over and kissed my cheek. "Was it like that with your family?"

I nodded. "They were always over, cooking, watching my cousins, building something. It was a little community. I haven't seen that in a long time. I forgot how much I missed it." I had a feeling my family was going to get bigger soon, though, so I vowed not to be sad for long.

———

Thirty minutes later, we walked into my apartment and flopped on the couch.

My ear twitched before I heard him. "Oh, you look plum tuckered out there, my bonny Hen."

I turned and saw Will sitting on the arm of the couch. "I am, but I'm fine."

"Hello, Will," Richard greeted the ghost like he always did after I said something to thin air.

He didn't take his eyes off me. "Hello, Detective."

I managed a little smile. "He says hello."

"What was it that made you so tired then?" He slid between me and the couch, and I bumped into Richard as he pushed me over a bit. Richard chuckled and kissed my forehead.

"Helping a shifter get a spell off him."

He looked mildly impressed at that. "Sounds dangerous."

I shrugged. "His pack was there. It helped. And Gwen."

He scoffed and got to his feet. "That purple headed witch who kicked me out of the precinct?" He crossed his arms and shook his, not looking at me. "I don't care to ever see her again."

"Ha! Well, she's coming over soon, so you be nice." I wagged my finger at him.

He turned, and his shoulders sank. He looked like a sulky teenager. "Hen! No!"

"Will! Yes!" My doorbell rang, and I patted Richard's arm before I got up and answered. Gwen and Hyde were in the hallway. He had managed to change into civvies, it seems, sporting a black t-shirt and jeans. He was holding bags of food, and Gwen had four large drinks in a carrier.

She had a big smile on her face as she walked in. "Hi!" Gwen lifted the drink carrier. "Brought some cheap Mexican, I always like that after I have to cast a big spell like that." Gwen set the drinks on the living room table, and Hyde put the stuffed bags down. I got some plates, and Gwen started pulling things out of the bags and piling them on the table.

"So, what'd ya bring?" I knew Richard had to be starving. Hell, I was too.

"Tacos, burritos, nachos, the works," Hyde said as he piled a plate with one of everything and handed it to Richard.

"Ooh, sounds good." Richard quickly pulled a crunchy taco out of its wrapper, and it was gone in two bites. We piled the non-traditional Mexican food on our plates, and soon, the air was filled with the sound of crunching.

"You." Gwen looked up, and so did I when I noticed Will pop back up behind the couch and was staring her down. His arms were still crossed, and he looked annoyed.

"Oh." She quickly swallowed her bite. "Hi, Will."

"My bonny Hen told me to be nice, but I haven't quite decided to yet," he said, motioning to her with a tilt of his head. I rolled my eyes, Will was never that good at being intimidating, but Gwen didn't know that.

"That's right, I did tell you that, so you better listen. She didn't realize what Ryan was doing."

Hyde looked around a second. "Wait, he's *here* now?" He said around a big bite of burrito.

I turned to Hyde. "Yes, he made his way over after Gwen banished him from the precinct."

"And I don't plan on leaving." He sat on the back of the couch, his arms crossed. It made the back of the couch sink a little, and Hyde jumped a bit from the invisible motion.

I held back my chuckle the best I could. "You don't have to leave."

Gwen put her taco back on her plate. "I really am sorry, Will, I just thought you were a passerby. I didn't think you lived there."

"Well, I did." He turned his nose up at her, and I once again fought a chuckle. "But if my bonny Hen says to be nice...I suppose I'll be nice."

I watched Gwen bite her lip at that, trying to hide a smile. "Thank you, I appreciate that." I noticed how Richard wasn't paying attention as he scarfed his taco, but Hyde was looking between us, like he had to, or someone would scold him.

"So, how's it going with Gwen?" I took a bite of my burrito, and it was okay, mostly beans and cheese. Hyde quickly looked at me and picked up the tomatoes that fell out of his taco, and put them back in.

"Going good, I'm learning a lot."

"Me too," Gwen said. "I feel like there's something new happening every day."

"Good." I turned to Richard, who was on his third taco, and I couldn't stop my little laugh. I picked up a cheese-covered chip and saw Gwen was holding the charm she had around her neck and was smiling as she looked at Richard. "What?" She looked over at me and was about to say something when something else caught her eye. She was looking between me, Will, and Richard. "What?" I chuckled and popped the nacho in my mouth.

She quickly let go of her charm. "Oh, uh, nothing."

"Naw, she saw something, lass," Will teased her.

I shook my head and sighed. "Clearly."

"You don't want to know?" Will walked over to her and

bent close to her ear. "I bet it's juicy."

I snickered. "Juicy?" Gwen and I both chuckled. "Where did you learn that one?"

"One of those awful shows you put on the TV and don't pay attention to."

I sipped my pop and shook my head. "That's it, History Channel from now on." Richard chuckled, and Hyde just tried not to seem uncomfortable as he turned to Richard.

"How long does it take for you to get used to hearing half a conversation?"

He laughed. "Depends on how long they are. Shorter conversations are easier. Ones like this are amusing to me now. Don't feel you have to pay attention. It's like any other conversation around you. If you hear it, you hear it," he said with a shrug.

Hyde nodded before his eyes went wide. "Oh, shit, I almost forgot." He got his phone out of his pocket. "You were spot on with that axe place Roa." I watched him open something in his photo gallery. "The first victims were there three days before Glass killed his girlfriend. And of course, our latest victims went there a lot." He handed me his phone, and I saw a pic from Glass' social media of him and his girlfriend smiling and holding axes at a familiar looking venue.

"Well, considering we met Olin at Solstice Axe throwing, I'd say that's another tick on the column that he's the one we saw in the house." I motioned to Gwen.

"You met at the axe place?" I nodded and handed Hyde back his phone. "I thought Mabon introduced you?" Richard was busy chewing, so he was no help. Shit.

"Uh, well, Nicola had a date with Mabon, and I wanted to make sure she'd be okay, and I asked Moss to come cause,

you know, big guy energy and all that." Oh man, that was the
dumbest reason that could have come out of my mouth.

"I met Mabon yesterday at his coffee shop," Gwen spoke
up. "He's nice." Gwen ate a cheese-covered chip. "Nicola showed
me a pic of them on her phone the other day. They look super
cute together."

I nodded and couldn't hide my smile. "Don't they? The
axe throwing was fun, but it'll probably be more fun when I can
throw with my dominant arm. I'm lucky I didn't throw the axe
into the floor." Gwen smiled in agreement, but I noticed Hyde
was giving Richard a look that said he wasn't totally buying what
I had to sell. Will bent down and smelled Gwen's nachos, so she
held them out for him.

"You don't eat this much, do ya, Hen?"

I brushed some crumbs off my fingers and picked up a taco.
"No, my abuela's cooking kind of ruined me for cheap Mexican
food. Even though it's been years since I've had any, I'll never
forget how it tasted." Her pozole was my favorite. Whatever she
did to the pork, it was like eating bacon flavored stew. I've never
found anything that tasted like it.

"I get that," Hyde took a drink. "My grandma made the
best peach cobbler. I haven't found an equal yet."

"We should do that soon." Moss picked up a second
burrito and took a bite.

"Do what?" I wadded up my taco papers and threw them
in one of the bags.

"Cook something your Abuela cooked when you were a
kid," he said around his bite. I sat back and thought for a moment.
My cousin never really let me cook. She was afraid I'd lose
control of my magic for some reason and set fire to the kitchen.
So, everything I learned to do was later, but it never seemed to

be as good.

"We could try, I suppose. I don't have any of her recipes, but I can find some online. I'm sure they'd be good too."

"How come you don't have any of your abuela's recipes?" Gwen looked sad for some reason, like I was truly missing out. I suppose, in a way, I was.

"My cousin has them all, and she took them when she left town."

"Oh! Well, they're not totally lost then. I'm sure she'd share." I appreciated her enthusiasm, but I knew differently.

I snickered. "Yeah, but I'd have to call her or something. I have a feeling she'd rather I didn't."

Richard shook his head. "She should give you copies of them. You deserve them." It wasn't like I disagreed, but after my cousin left, I think I could count on one hand how many times I'd heard from her. She didn't even invite me to her wedding.

"What about you, Will?" Gwen looked up at him. "Do you remember any favorite foods when you were alive?" I tried to hide my smile as she got to know him. I had a feeling he was loving all the attention as he sat on the corner of her chair and held his chin.

"Hmm, I do miss a good crowdie."

I giggled. "And what is a crowdie?" Both Richard and Hyde's eyes went wide at that, clearly we were all in the dark with that one.

He smiled and started walking around us. "Oh, it's got cream and oatmeal and honey. When the harvest was good, you'd get raspberries in it, and my wife would always—" He stopped. A haunted look came over his face as he just stood still.

"Will?"

Richard looked over at us. "Something wrong?"

I shook my head. "I don't know, he just stopped."

Gwen stood and walked over to him. "Will, you all right?"

He ignored her and looked at me. "My wife would always put more whiskey in it than was necessary, but I loved her for that." His voice was quiet and mournful.

Gwen's eyes went sad. "You were married?" He nodded and went invisible. Seems he was starting to remember more about his past.

"He was married?" Hyde looked around even though he couldn't see him.

"He knew he was married," I told them. "But I think he just remembered something about her. It shook him up."

"Poor guy." Hyde watched as Gwen sat back down. "Is he still here?"

She shrugged. "If he is, he doesn't want us to see him."

I sighed and finished another taco. "He'll come back. He always does."

———

An hour later, Gwen and Hyde left, the four of us sufficiently stuffed. Will never showed back up, and I hoped whatever he remembered about his wife wasn't too sad.

"That was nice of them to bring dinner." Richard picked up the empty bags and got to his feet.

"It was. We'll have to do it next time."

He smiled. "Deal." I picked up the empty drink cups and walked them to the kitchen. "You've been doing a lot of raw magic lately, haven't you?" I was surprised he knew what that was and smiled.

"I have, how'd you know?"

He followed behind me and leaned on the counter. "I've been reading up on witches and their magic. It said if you don't light a candle or use other things to do a spell, you know, like your happy face blood bag," I snickered. "It's raw magic, straight from wherever magic comes from."

I turned and smiled at him. "That's true."

"I just want to make sure you aren't wearing yourself out since you asked for fire during the spell earlier."

I pulled him down to my lips and gave him a little kiss. "I'm fine, I promise, but thank you for worrying. Do you want to stay over tonight?" *Please, please, please.*

He stepped up close to me. "Wild horses couldn't drag me away." His voice was low like it was that one morning, and I couldn't stop the little gasp that escaped my lips as he lifted me in his arms and set me on the kitchen counter.

"Richard Marie Moss!"

He roared with laughter and hugged me close. "That is not my middle name." He snaked between my legs.

"I know, but that's what I came up with." I kissed his cheek. "What is your middle name?" He kissed my lips over and over, just little soft pecks that drove me wild.

"Callan," he said between kisses.

My eyes went wide at that one. "Callan, never heard that name before." Or had I? It sounded vaguely familiar, but I didn't know anyone with that name.

"Family name. What's yours?" He kissed my neck, and I smiled.

"Valeria."

He leaned back, a little smile on his face. "Damn, Lily Valeria Roa, that is quite a name."

"You think so?" He nodded and gave me a kiss.

"I do." His fingers worked their way under my shirt. He ran his lips along my cheek and kissed my neck as his arms tightened around me. I leaned my head to the right and let him kiss every inch of my neck before he moved to the other side, kissing as he went. His lips tickled my skin, and thankfully, I kept the giggles to myself. When he got to the other side, his lips gave way to teeth as he gently bit the skin at my pulse and sucked. I didn't hold back then and let him hear how much I liked that. My moan came in tandem with my fingers tightening against his arms.

"I love how you do that," I whispered as his arms pulled me closer.

"You know what I love?" His voice had that husky growl that drove me crazy. His fingers went from my back to the button on my jeans.

"What?" I watched him unbutton the five buttons on my jeans and slide his hands in them around my ass. I had to admit it was impressive.

His lips brushed my ear, and his words made me shiver. "The sound you make when my tongue licks your clit." He lifted me just a bit and pulled my jeans off. I couldn't stop the little yelp that came out of my mouth. But I laughed as he threw them on the floor and pulled me closer to the edge of the counter.

"We are in the kitchen, good sir."

He chuckled. "Yeah, but it's our kitchen," he kissed me, and I felt his hands sneak their way between my skin and my underwear. "We know where we've been." I couldn't help but laugh again.

"Men." He slipped my underwear down my legs, and I gave a little gasp as my bare ass hit the cold counter. "Cold!"

He laughed and kissed my knee. "Sorry, Sweetheart," he kissed his way up my leg. "I'm sure you won't feel it much longer." His arms went around me as he laid me back against the counter, and I felt him kiss his way back down my leg. I broke out in goosebumps as he kissed my hips a second before I felt his tongue run up my middle. I gasped as my feet landed on his shoulders. His tongue was almost lazy as he ran it around my clit. Slow, deep waves of pleasure ran through me.

Normally, I would run my fingers through his hair, but I couldn't reach him, not like this, so my fingers gripped the edge of the counter. His hand slid up my torso and cupped my breast, his fingers pinched my nipple as he sucked, and I couldn't stop the cry that came from me. His lips and tongue were perfect on me, and before I realized it was building, my orgasm rocked me, and I felt my hips rise off the counter. Wave after wave of pleasure spread through me, and after one last lick, he stood above me. He had that wicked smile on his glistening lips, and I wrapped my arms around him.

"Shall we take this into the bedroom?"

He chuckled. "You read my mind." He lifted me off the counter and carried me through the apartment as I kissed his neck, eager for whatever else he had planned.

CHAPTER 8

"So, he's definitely the one you saw in the homes, telling people to kill their significant other?" Late the next morning, we found ourselves in Ryan's office, explaining how far we were on the case. It helped that we knew who the fae was now and that she was making Olin do her dirty work. Now we just had to find her.

"Yes, sir," Richard said. "But he was compelled to do so as Ms. Roa said, and her report will reflect that." He motioned at the stack of papers that Ryan was flipping through.

The Major nodded. "Well, good work. Now we gotta find that fae." He looked between us.

"Yes, sir." We got to our feet, and Richard shook his hand before we walked back to our desks.

"That's going to be the tricky bit." I turned to Gwen and Hyde who were sitting at their respective desks. "My fae contact said she already tried to find Eldora but couldn't. If they can't find her, there's not a lot of hope that we can."

"You don't think she's going to go after Olin again, do you?" Hyde asked.

I shrugged. "I can't begin to understand her train of thought, but if she does, she'll find his mind unavailable. We'll see how she reacts to that." I looked over at Gwen. "Best put some extra protections around your home just in case."

"Will do," she said with a nod.

"Do you think this fae could retaliate against us?" I could

see Richard looked worried.

"If she finds out who we are, maybe." I did worry that since she tried to drain me while I was trying to get the spell off Olin, she knew who I was. So, all I could do was prepare for the worst. "She's clearly not in her right mind. But I'll make sure we're protected. Plus, there's Will at my place. He's like the best kind of guard dog. One who doesn't sleep."

Richard laughed and turned back to his computer. "True."

"Have you heard from Glass's attorney?" I asked Richard.

"Yeah, his preliminary hearing is next week," he said without turning. "We should go."

"Okay." I chewed on my thumbnail, a habit I really needed to break. "Are they going to ask us questions?"

"I doubt it. This is just to see if there's enough evidence to go to trial. And technically, there is." He turned in his chair, "That's where we'll shine in his defense." I nodded and turned back to my desk. I half expected Will to pop up on my desk, but then I remembered he was at home. I hoped he wasn't moping, he tended to throw things around, and I didn't want to clean up after him.

I laid my hands on my desk with a little bang. "I'm going to see Nicola."

"Okay, want to get some BBQ for lunch?" That sounded amazing, and my mouth immediately watered at the thought.

I turned to him as I stood. "Ooh, yeah, good choice." He gave me a wink, and I walked down to the morgue. I rounded the corner and saw Nicola showing Laurette where everything was kept. She must have heard my footsteps because she turned before I said anything.

"Lily!" I laughed and walked over to them. She had a huge smile on her face and definitely had something to tell me.

"Nicola!" I teased and leaned on the clean morgue table.

"Guess what," she reached over the table and grabbed my arms. "Mabon and I have another date tonight."

"Hell yeah!" The two of us laughed while Laurette turned, trying to hide her own smile. "Where are you going?"

She stood and crossed her arms. Her shoulders wiggled as she spoke. "Little intimate dinner at Intermezzo's, then some ice cream."

"And then?" I heard Laurette chuckle behind her.

"And then?" She sighed happily, staring at nothing as she spoke. "I'm gonna throw that giant man in my bed and never let him go." The three of us laughed.

"She has been telling me of Mabon," Laurette finally turned to us. "He seems like a good man."

"He is. He's had a crush on Nicola for years. I'm so glad she's finally given him a chance." I gave her arm a little poke.

"Me too. Should have done it sooner."

"Well, just think of all the ways you can catch up with him," I snickered.

"Oh, I am." We all laughed again, and I turned to Laurette. Her dark hair was still in a bun behind her head, and she was wearing black running shoes instead of heels like Nicola usually wore.

"So, how are you liking Arion?"

Laurette smiled. "It's a cozy little place. I like it so far. It's a thing to get used to, though, traveling to another town for something."

I smiled. "Yeah, it's small here, and the town mayor is always a hard ass about building new stores. We're all just used to it, so nobody really tries too hard."

She pointed at Nicola, her finger bobbing as she spoke. "I

do like the coffee shop that Mabon owns. His drinks are really good."

"Aren't they?" I nudged Nicola, who smiled. "We were all glad when he moved into that space. It makes it harder for the town to say, 'No you can't have that' when the space is already there."

"What was there before?" Laurette leaned on the table with us.

"It used to be a boarding house in the thirties. I think that's when it was built." My fingers drummed on my chin as I tried to remember what I knew about that area of town. "Then a hotel for a bit before it closed down. His place was empty for years, though, I think he lives above it?" I looked over at Nicola, who nodded.

Laurette looked over at Nicola. "Is his business haunted? I heard boarding places are notorious for having a bad past."

Nichola turned to me, her arms crossed. "I don't know, not really my forte."

I shrugged. "If there are ghosts there, they haven't made themselves known, and Mabon never said anything."

"Hmm, maybe they are happy."

I nodded. "Could be. So, Moss and I were going to get BBQ for lunch. Would you two like to join us?"

Laurette smiled. "I've never had American BBQ. I'd love to."

"You know me and meat," Nicola gave me a nudge. "We'll be ready in a sec."

"Okay." I took the elevator back up to the bullpen and saw Richard pulling his suit jacket off the coat rack. "Nicola and Laurette are going to join us." I saw Gwen and Hyde were gone. "Where'd they go?"

He turned and put his suit jacket on. "Got a call, something about a possessed toy."

I laughed. "Nine times out of ten, it's the batteries dying. Guess it'll just be the four of us." I grabbed my purse and put it across my chest.

"Lunch with three beautiful women, I could do worse." I scoffed and hit his chest. He walked closer to me. "Of course, you are the most beautiful."

My cheeks heated at that, and it was a losing battle as I tried to hide my smile. "Boy, hush, someone will hear." He laughed as we walked into the elevator. When the door shut, he quickly wrapped his arms around me and kissed me until the door started opening. "You're in a playful mood."

"I'll show you what kind of mood I'm in later," he whispered in my ear and gave my ass a little smack as I walked out of the elevator. I was quite sure my face was as red as it had ever been.

"Hey, Seattle," Nicola teased as she and Laurette walked over. "Lily, tell you about my next date?"

He smiled as we walked out to his car. "No, you'll have to tell me."

"Are you from Seattle?" Laurette asked as we climbed into his car. The three of us laughed as he pulled out onto the street.

———

We sat at a booth at Fiery Pig BBQ and ordered our lunch while Laurette continued to get to know us. "So you're from Oregon," she pointed at Richard. "But she calls you Seattle." Her finger landed on Nicola.

"Yes," Richard smiled. "Busting balls is something you learn by hanging around police officers. At least here in America."

She chuckled. "I see. So, how long have you been in

Arion?"

He looked over at me. "Oh, eight months?"

I nodded. "Sounds about right."

"And how long have you two been together?" I sat straight in shock, and so did Richard.

"What?" I was not as eloquent as him under pressure sometimes.

"You mean, how long have we been partners?" Fuck, of course that's what she meant, right?

"Well, depends on how you mean partners. You are lovers, yes? I don't think I've ever seen someone with such red cheeks after coming out of an elevator." She winked, and I almost choked, holding back a laugh. It was Richard's turn to lose his cool as Nicola tried to hide her smile under her hand.

"Oh uh, no," he looked at me, and I shook my head. "No, we're not, we're just work partners."

Laurette snickered and took a drink of her tea. "I take it you're not supposed to be together?"

"Probably not." But of course, I made it sound like a question, so that didn't help.

Laurette smiled at us. "You know my great-grandmother was fae."

My eyes went wide. "Really?" That didn't surprise me. There were more fae/human couples in Europe than there were in the States. Plus, she was gorgeous.

"Mm-hmm, and she passed a unique ability to me." She laid her elbows on the table and smiled. "I can always tell when someone is lying to me." My jaw dropped, and I froze. We were definitely caught. "My mother always said I was wasting my abilities on the dead instead of the living."

"Is that so?" Richard turned to me. I was still in shock to

react much. "I think we're caught Sweetheart." Nicola giggled as her hands wrapped around her drink.

"Don't tell Ryan. Matter of fact don't tell anyone else. We aren't exactly sure if they'd let us date or not, and I don't want to mess up our jobs." Richard kissed my head, and I leaned into him. It really was the only black spot hanging over our heads. Would our relationship mess up our careers or not?

Laurette waved my concern away. "Don't worry, forbidden love is always worth it and much sexier." I looked up at Richard, and he gave my forehead a kiss. "You're cute together," Laurette teased.

"Thank you." The waiter brought our food, I got BBQ bologna, beans, and cornbread. Richard got ribs, corn on the cob, and coleslaw. Nicola got a pulled pork sandwich, and Laurette, never having American BBQ before, got a sample platter of four kinds of meat and beans.

"You gonna eat all that?" Nicola teased as she pointed to the big plate.

She picked up her fork and speared some brisket. "Depends on how good it is."

———

I was impressed with how Laurette almost finished her lunch, but with only a few bites left, she admitted defeat. At least she said it was amazing and couldn't wait to have it again. It reminded me of how I introduced Nicola to a bunch of new food when she moved to town. We had fun trying out a lot of things, from biscuits and gravy to chicken fried steak. Maybe the two of us could do that with Laurette. Food and girl time always appealed to me. Laurette also assured us that she would keep our relationship a secret, which we both appreciated. When we got back to the precinct, we took the elevator back upstairs. I saw

Gwen reading one of the Fell's books at her desk. I walked over and leaned against her desk, but she didn't notice me.

"Possessed toy or battery?"

She looked up with a gasp. "Oh!" She chuckled, "Sorry you startled me. Battery." We smiled, and I looked over at Richard.

"Told ya." He smiled and logged into his computer.

"Yeah, new mom, sleep-deprived. She just got a little spooked. All is well now." She went back to the book.

"Whatcha reading?"

"Looking into more of that bonding spell you found."

"Yeah? Anything interesting?" But I didn't hear her. My eyes glanced at her desk, and I saw the file for what happened at the mansion last fall. While I had given my version of events, from what I could remember, I had never read it. Never even asked Nicola or Richard to elaborate on the day. But Gwen was reading it or at least planned to. "Have you read that yet?" I interrupted her as I pointed to the file. She moved the book and picked it up.

"Yeah, rough stuff." She handed it to me, but I didn't take it. "Do you want to read it?" She sounded hesitant, and I stared at it for a moment. "You might find it healing." I knew she was right, and it wasn't like I relished having holes in my memories. I didn't remember anything from right before my arm got lopped off to maybe a week or two later in the hospital. I knew reading it would be rough, so I had put it off. I looked back at Richard, he was talking to another officer, and I knew if he were there while I read it, everything would be okay.

I reached out and took the file. "It could be." She shut the book and laid it on my desk as I stared at the file.

My ear twitched, and I felt Richard behind me. "Oh, I see." He took the file from me. "Did you want to read it?"

I took a breath. "I think I should." I turned, and he was a lot closer than he usually was when we were around other officers. "I went to the store, so I have more things for dinner."

He nodded. "I'll cook, you read?" I nodded, and we sat back at our desks. He put the file on mine, and I stared at it a moment.

"You know," Gwen leaned against my desk. "You could always talk to Ryan about that day too."

I grimaced at the thought. "True, but why?"

She shrugged. "You both went through something traumatic that day. And I know you don't particularly like him, but it could be a step in the right direction?" I grumbled like an angry cat and turned to the Major's office. He was alone, typing something on his computer, and the door was open. "You have therapy later today, right?" I nodded and turned back to her. "Think of how cathartic that will be after talking to him."

I couldn't help myself and laughed. "True." I sighed and heard Richard's chair squeak.

"She's right. It might be a good idea."

I groaned again. "You all are just ganging up on me."

"Yep!" Gwen smiled and patted my arm before she sat back at her desk. I turned back to Richard. He was sitting back in his chair, his fingers laced over his stomach.

"Up to you."

"Yeah." I looked back at Ryan's office. He was still alone. I steeled myself and walked over, ignoring the stares I usually got when I went to Ryan's office. I knocked on the door. "Major?"

He looked over from his computer. "Roa, what can I do for you?" I walked in and took a seat across from him. He turned and laced his hands on the desk.

"I uh...I know I haven't asked before, but it has been

brought to my attention that the day the Fells died was a bad day for everyone, and I was wondering if there might be anything you could tell me about the day that wouldn't be in the report?"

He sat back, putting his hands on the arms of his chair. "Have you read it yet?" I shook my head. "Me either. Not since I gave my testimony." I could have sworn I saw a haunted look in his eyes. "My wife is always telling me to have a sit down with you about that day, but I'm a chicken shit sometimes."

I gave a little chuckle at that. "Gwen and Moss have said the same, that I should talk to you."

He nodded. "Well, if you have some time, close the door, and I'll tell you what happened." I got up and quietly closed the door and sat back down, readying myself for a hard conversation.

―――――

An hour later, he shook my hand, and I walked out of his office. My mind was going wild with what he told me. I wanted to read the report and put everything together, see if my mind wanted to remember any of that awful night. But first therapy. I walked over to Richard, who was all ready to go.

"Time for therapy?" I nodded, and we headed towards the elevator. "How was the talk?"

"Oh, it was…informative." I was glad he didn't ask me to elaborate. I wasn't sure I was ready to talk about what I just learned.

―――――

Gwen was right. Therapy was cathartic, even if Ryan and I didn't end up yelling at each other. I was almost as tired as I was after the first day, but I was proud of myself for not falling asleep in the car on the way to my apartment. I sat in my big, comfy chair and read the file as Richard made what was sure to be a masterpiece in the kitchen. I quickly skimmed to the bits I didn't remember when I felt cold hands on my shoulders.

"Why you readin' that Hen?"

I looked up at Will, and his eyes locked onto mine. "I need to know what happened. I spoke with Ryan earlier, and I figured it was time."

"Hello, Will." I smiled as Richard called out to the ghost from the kitchen.

"Hello, Detective." He sat on the arm of the chair.

"He says hello." My eyes found the start of what I didn't remember, and I stopped for a moment. It was now or never. I took a deep breath and read on. I wondered how it would differ, listening to Ryan tell me what happened to what he wrote in the report.

When we pulled up to the house, we saw Officers Greggs and Dennis unconscious on the ground, Dennis had wounds in his chest from what looked like wooden shrapnel, and Greggs had burns on his face and hands. Officers Brooks and Collins rendered first aid to the best of their ability before the medics loaded them up into separate ambulances. The front door was destroyed, and from the bits of wood scattered on the porch and yard, it was clear something powerful had blown it to bits from the inside.

When we reached the porch, we could all hear Roa yelling inside the house, so we ran in. First thing we encountered was Det. Moss unconscious on the floor with a bullet wound in his left arm. Officer Hyde quickly applied a tourniquet, and he regained consciousness. Officers Lennox, Ravi, Montgomery, and Pine checked the other bodies around the room. Two were still alive and taken into custody, while the others were marked as deceased. Their identities will be determined later. I, along with Officers Fitzroy, Vale, and Hawthorne, ran into the room where we could hear Roa. As we entered, we saw Ms. Roa was in the room, as well as an older Caucasian male. Roa was on her knees, clearly casting a spell as the other man in the room looked to be choking. Next to Roa was a suit of armor that was holding a bloody sword. I then saw what looked like an arm on the floor, and I quickly realized it was Roa's.' I remember what Ryan said about this bit.

"I saw your arm on the ground, and I couldn't fucking believe it." He didn't look at me as he spoke, just held his chin as he shook his head.

"Which part?"

He scoffed. "One, that there was an arm on the ground to begin with. Two, that it was yours, and three, you were still casting that spell on the bad guy." He sighed and ran his hand over his hair. "But I knew that if you were casting a spell on that other guy, he had to be bad news. So, I didn't hesitate to tell the other officers to open fire. I had hoped that if he went down, whatever was in that suit of armor would go down too because I had a feeling bullets weren't really going to work on it." He scooted forward in his chair. "What exactly was in that suit of armor?" That didn't surprise me. He said he didn't read the report, meaning he didn't know my side of it either.

"A dead body."

His eyes went wide. "Just a...regular old dead body?"

I nodded. "No need to be special to be a revenant. I'm not sure where he got it, though. I don't remember any cemeteries being raided around that time." That's when something occurred to me. "Oh shit."

"What?"

"I think he'd been lugging that revenant around wherever he went. That would account for no other bodies missing."

Ryan shook his head and sat back. "Never thought of

that."

"Nor me, until now. I can see we should have had this little talk a while ago."

"Well, my wife is rather smart." I smiled a little at that.

I ordered everyone to fire at the man in the room, and after two hits, which were determined to be from Officer Fitzroy, the man went down, as did the suit of armor, and Roa collapsed to the floor. I ran next to her and could see she was barely conscious.

I vaguely remember Ryan being in the room, and surprised he wasn't yelling at me.

I picked her up, pressing the wound to my chest as I ran her outside to an ambulance, telling Officer Hawthorne to get her arm and follow me. When I ran outside, I saw two more ambulances had arrived, and I quickly ran her over to one. The medics could see I needed a stretcher and worked fast, so by the time I reached them, I was able to put Roa on it. I rode with Roa to the hospital, holding pressure on the wound while the medic started an I.V. and took her vitals.

When I was in his office, this part chilled me. "I had never seen anyone bleed so much, and I was really scared we were going to lose you. When I picked you up, I pressed you as hard as I could to my chest to try and stop it. I knew after my monumental fuck up, I had to do everything I could to make sure you were gonna make it. The ambulance ride was so long that I swore you were getting paler by the minute. I had so many gauzes pressed to your arm, but it really didn't seem to help." I saw a haunted look in his eyes, like that day was the worst for the entire department.

The medics were able to keep her arm cold until we reached the hospital, where it was immediately put on ice. Soon after, Det Moss, Officer Greggs, and Dennis were brought in and assessed. Moss was treated for a gunshot wound in his left bicep and a few lacerations to the face and neck. Greggs and Dennis were treated for burns, slight concussions, and puncture wounds. All three will recover and return to duty soon. Thirty minutes after Roa arrived at the hospital, she went into surgery to reattach her arm. The doctors are fairly confident she will regain the use of it and will be able to return to duty.

"You know I never liked that Ryan," I felt Will's hand on my shoulder. "But he really helped you."

"He did." Even after he told me this afternoon, my memory was still refusing to remember much. The rest of the report was written by another officer who stayed at the scene.

After those who were injured were taken to the hospital, the remaining ambulance helped stabilize the cult members who were still alive. The medical examiner, Dr. Nicola Stroud, gathered the bodies of the dead cult members as well as Jackson and Amelia Fell. Dr. Stroud took great care in moving their bodies, as all of Jackson and about half of Amelia's body were somehow transmuted into a green goo-like substance.

Officers Hawthorne and Dove were able to wake the two suspects and put them in the back of their patrol cars. Unfortunately, when they were left alone, they committed suicide by what was determined later as ingesting cyanide that was hidden in one of their teeth. The same method as another suspect that had earlier been arrested for breaking into Lily Roa's apartment.

I started to smell food, and my stomach rumbled. "What are you making for dinner? It smells good."

"Thanks, pesto chicken with toasted rice and zucchini."

I smiled. "Mmm, you spoil me."

"You deserve it." My ear twitched because Richard and Will had said that at the same time. I gave Will a little nudge, and he slid down beside me. His cold arm went around my shoulders. "I cannae believe that's what happened to you, Hen. That sounds like a nightmare." I sat still, Will's arm around me, and I wondered if I'd ever truly remember what happened.

"I know, it does." I felt his cold hand on my scar, the magic making my skin tingle.

"I never came across a revenant a'fore. They sound terrifyin'."

I laid my head on his shoulder, and my cheek quickly turned cold. "Most death magic is. To bring any semblance of life to a dead body is an atrocity that should be punished by whatever gods there are."

His fingers ran up and down my arm. "You cannae bring a person back, can ye?"

I shook my head. "No, not really. All the spells I know only animate dead bodies. There's never any soul in it, and they only remember who they were for a short time. Then they're mindless husks."

"What about fae magic?" Richard called out from the kitchen. "Is it different from what you do?" I knew fae magic was the same. They just had more time to cultivate it, so it always seemed more powerful. Hell, it was in the long run.

I sat up and turned to the kitchen so he could hear me. "As far as I know, it's the same, just more connected to the earth and more powerful because they're old."

"I remember an old story," I turned back to Will, and he tucked some hair behind my ear. "An elven lass lost her love, and she searched the world for a way to bring him back. One day, she came across Death and asked for his help. Death said there's nothing can be done. His soul is passed on. That there was a way of doing things, and if they were upset, dreadful things would happen." He ran his knuckles along my cheek, and there was something in his eyes that was familiar. But if I remembered what it was, it would make me cry. "But she wanted her love back, consequences be damned. So, she stole the pendant around Death's neck and went about trying to summon the soul of her love."

"Let me guess, it didn't work."

He shook his head. "Nope. Death caught up with her, took his pendant back, and punished her. He cursed the elf so that no matter how long she lived, her love would never find her. She would never find him. They'd be separated by anything and everything."

My heart broke a little for the elf, who probably never existed. "Harsh."

The corner of his mouth tilted in a little smile. "Some say it wasn't enough because of the damage she could have caused. But aye, it was harsh. Especially for an immortal." I shivered a little from his hand on me, and he finally took it off my cheek. "But I understand. If my wife died before me, I'd do anything to get her back."

I clicked my tongue and held his hand. "Are you starting to remember more about her?"

He nodded and looked down at our hands. "Aye, I am." He ran his free fingers over my hand.

"Do you want to talk about her?"

He stared into my eyes for a moment. "Her name was Rhoswen, it means white rose. She was the most beautiful lass I'd ever laid my undeserving eyes on." Well, he was really laying it on thick now, and I couldn't stop my little smile.

"Was it love at first sight?"

He barked out a laugh. "No, I annoyed her, I know. We grew up together. I was friends with her brothers. When we were sixteen, there was a sickness that swept through the village. Her Da and her brothers died, so it was just her and her Ma, so I helped them around their farm until it was up to snuff, so to say, and her Ma could sell it. It gave them a fair bit o'coin, so they moved into a house in the village. She wanted to thank me for the help, but I told her I'd do anything for her and that thanks were not needed." He sighed. "That must have done something because she kissed me, and there was no going back from there."

I smiled. "That's a sweet story."

"Tis." His eyes looked up. "Seems dinner is ready, you enjoy Hen." He kissed my cheek and disappeared. I turned and saw Richard coming over with two plates.

"Dinner," he said with a smile.

"Smells good. I'm starving." He set the plates down, and I joined him on the couch. The chicken was covered with homemade pesto sauce, and the rice was soaking up the juices from the zucchini. "Thank you." I leaned over and gave him a kiss.

"You're welcome, Sweetheart." I took a bite of the chicken, and it was juicy and perfect, and the pesto was fresh and nutty. "So, what were you and Will talking about?"

"His wife." I told him what Will told me.

"I hope him remembering more won't hurt him." I looked over, and he put a few slices of zucchini in his mouth.

"No, I think it'll be healing. Isn't that what therapists say anyway?" I speared a few slices of zucchini with my fork and ate them. I never liked zucchini until Richard made it for me a few months ago. But the way he made it, I couldn't resist it.

"True."

After dinner, I perused through some more books while Richard took a shower. It was another of the Fell's books. Reading them really made me feel closer to them. I ran my hand over the page and closed my eyes. *Why would a fae want a man in mourning to do her dirty work? Why would she involve her love's brother in such a scheme? What good would it do her?* I felt magic tingling in my fingers, and I opened my eyes. I saw a bright light coming from one of the boxes, and before I could move, a brightly lit book started floating over to me.

"Thanks, Will." I grabbed the book and started flipping through it.

My ear twitched as he spoke without becoming corporeal. "Welcome, Hen." I flipped through the pages until I saw the light. The second I touched it, the page went dark. It was a spell that dealt with death magic. As I read it, my eyes went wide. I couldn't believe it.

"Find something?" I looked up at Richard. He was standing in the doorway of the bedroom, a towel around his waist and using another to rub his hair dry.

The corner of my mouth went up in a snicker. "Yes but looking at you like that is going to make me forget."

He chuckled and sat next to me. "Ooh, death magic." His happy face turned worried, as would anyone's.

"Yeah, and I think I found out why Eldora put that spell on Olin."

"Oh yeah?"

I put my finger on the page and read aloud. "Using one whose heart is in mourning to kill three people whose heart is full of exaltation can create a 'Calamaris,' a being pulled from the pits that can be used to find souls. But a Calamaris is unstable. If the summoner cannot control it, the being will start pulling souls from living beings." I looked back up at Richard. "When she has that magic, Eldora can use it to find Dimitri's soul in the afterlife."

"Shit. You think she can control it?"

I sat back and sighed. "I wouldn't bet against her."

"So, what do you think she's planning?"

I looked down at the book and tried not to shiver at the thought. "Well, Dimitri doesn't have a body anymore, so that's her next roadblock. My assumption is, if she were successful in killing three people, she would find Dimitri's soul, take Olin's soul out, and put Dimitri's in. Thus, being reunited."

His eyes went wide. "She could do that?" He sounded horrified, and I didn't blame him.

"Since Olin's soul is mourning, it's more susceptible to magic. If she wanted to remove his soul and put Dimitri's in, it wouldn't take much." He sighed, shaking his head, making little droplets fall on the couch. "I did not put a spell on him for *that*."

He reached out and laid a hand on my shoulder. "At least you got that first spell off him."

"Yeah." I looked back down at the spell. "This is bad. This spell is only used by the desperate, and a desperate elf is a problem."

Richard sat back, tossing his towel over the arm of the couch. "Any way to get ahold of our other friend?"

"Yes, but..."

He sat forward, putting his elbows on his legs. "You don't

want to bug her?"

I pointed at him. "Bingo."

Richard looked at the book and read a few lines. "Is she going to have to start over now that you took that spell off him?"

I quickly skimmed through the pages again and sighed in relief. "Yes, the two involved have to be bound, so hopefully, either us or the fae can find her before she finds another poor soul to torture."

I was kneeling on the ground, my spell cutting off the man's air. *It shouldn't take so long!* I thought. *Why isn't he dead yet!* I could feel my energy draining every moment that went by. *Die, please die!* Something moved in my periphery, and before I could move, the suit of armor that was in the corner was next to me. What the fuck! I watched as it raised its sword, and my heart stuttered in my chest. "No!" I screamed and managed to tilt to my left just enough that the sword missed me. My shoulder felt cold, and I looked over. My eyes could hardly comprehend what they were seeing. Blood poured down my side, and on the floor was my arm. I guess the sword didn't miss after all. I looked back at the man who killed my friends. He was turning purple. I just had to keep this spell up for a moment longer. Then, whatever was in the armor could do whatever it wanted to me. But I had to kill this man for Jackson and Amelia. Hell for Howard, too.

Explosions sounded around me as the man shuddered, and blood bloomed on his shirt. Bullet holes, I realized, and put my arm down to stop the spell. I looked up, the yellow eyes in the suit of armor, staring at me a moment before the magic fled the body, and it fell to the ground.

"Roa!" It sounded like Ryan, and I fell to the ground. I was so fucking tired. All I wanted to do was sleep. "Don't worry, Roa,

I got you."

I sat up with a gasp, my left hand going to my right shoulder. It was there, attached like it had been for months. My heart was going a mile a minute as my dream flashed through my mind. I had never dreamed about that day, but it was as upsetting as being there. I looked over at Richard, and he was asleep on his side, breathing deeply. I needed some warm milk, so I quietly snuck out of bed and walked into the kitchen, still holding my shoulder.

My arms broke out in goosebumps as I reached for the fridge handle. "Had a nightmare, didn't ya Hen?" Will appeared next to the sink. His eyes looked worried.

"Yeah, about…that day." I opened the fridge and pulled out the milk. I watched as Will floated a mug down to me.

"You've never dreamed of it?" I shook my head and poured the milk into the mug and popped it into the microwave for forty-five seconds. When I took my hand back, it was shaking.

"I think reading the report unlocked some stuff." Will nodded. "It…I…" The microwave beeping startled me, and I opened it. Will floated the mug over to the table and set it on a coaster.

"Don't want you to burn yourself."

I hugged myself and sat on the couch. "Thanks." I scooted back into the corner, the cushions squeezing me comfortably. "I remembered that I moved."

Will appeared next to me, his hand on my knee. "You moved?"

I nodded. "I moved out of the way. If I didn't, that revenant would have killed me, its sword would have split my head. But I moved, and it only got my arm."

His eyes went wide as he hugged me. "Oh Hen, I could have lost ya." He was cold against my body. "I don't want to lose ya."

"I don't want to lose me either."

He chuckled and handed me the mug of milk. "Drink up, Hen." I took it from him and took a few deep swallows. The warm milk was soothing, an interesting contrast to the cold I felt from Will. I looked over at him, and that odd familiar feeling that my mind wouldn't let me remember floated in my mind.

"What is so familiar about you?"

His eyebrows went up. "Familiar?"

"Yeah, ever since you moved in, something familiar has been teasing at my memories, but I can't remember what it is." I finished my milk as he gave it some thought, holding his chin.

"I...cannae say, Hen." He reached out and tucked some hair behind my ear. There was something in his tone.

"Can't, or won't?"

He smiled. "You were always too smart for your own good Hen." He turned back to the bedroom a moment before I heard footsteps. "Seems you were missed, Hen." He went invisible and I saw Richard walk into the living room.

"You okay?" He sat next to me and gave my cheek a kiss.

I was quiet for a moment as I tried to gather my thoughts. "I remember." Richard clicked his tongue and pulled me onto his lap. His body was warm and snuggled against him. "I almost died."

His hand ran softly down my hair. "I know."

"No I mean," I sat up and held his face. "I almost died, I was almost split in two, but I moved just enough it only got my arm."

His eyes went wide. "Holy shit." He pulled me into

another hug, and I could feel his arms shaking. "That's insane."

"I wish Jackson and Amelia could have moved. Maybe they'd still be here." A tear ran down my cheek and over Richard's shoulder.

"Don't dwell, Sweetheart. It won't help." He was right of course, survivor's guilt was a real thing and something I had talked with Gloria about quite a bit when I first started seeing her. But I missed my friends and would for the rest of my life. "Let's go back to bed." I nodded, and he picked me up, princess style, and walked back into the bedroom. He laid me down on the bed and covered me up before sliding under the covers himself, wrapping his arms around me. "I love you, Lily, I'll forever be grateful that you moved."

"I love you too, Richard." The warm milk, and warm love next to me helped my mind settle, and I was able to go back to sleep. But not before I felt cold lips on my cheek, give me a quick peck.

CHAPTER 9

The next morning, I told Gwen and Hyde what I figured out about the Calamaris. Going over the creature and what it did was helping keep my newfound memories away. I didn't want to think about them while at work.

Gwen sat back in her chair. She looked pale. "I couldn't imagine being so..." She swallowed hard. "That's dark."

"It is. We got really lucky to have met Olin when we did. She's going to have to start over, and hopefully, we can get to her first."

Hyde nodded and gave Gwen a pat on the back. "Well, let us know if you need some help, we're up for it."

Gwen steeled herself when she looked back up at me. "We are."

"I know you are," I started to turn when I remembered. "Malin!"

Gwen jumped and chuckled. "What about her?"

"Who's Malin?" Hyde asked, an amused smile on his face.

"My familiar." Gwen pulled out her phone and showed him a picture.

"Aw, cute cat," he said as he sat at his desk.

Gwen turned back to me, and I leaned down on her desk. "Can she contact the fae for us? I already contacted them once without an invitation, and I'm not sure she'll be super excited to see me so soon. Despite what I've learned."

Gwen nodded. "Yeah, I think she'll love it. I haven't gotten her out of the house much lately."

I clapped my hands together once. "Great! Can we go now?" We both looked at our partners, who nodded.

"Yeah, go for it," Richard gave my arm a tap. "If something comes up, we'll just meet you two there."

"Perfect," I turned back to Gwen, who got to her feet. "Can I hold her in her car?"

Gwen laughed. "Yeah, she hates her carrier."

"Awesome, kitty snuggles." I turned back to Richard, who was laughing. "I'll let you know what happens."

"Good luck."

———

We picked up Malin, who was ecstatic about getting out of the house, and I gave Gwen the directions to the same hiking trail I took Richard to the other night. It was around ten in the morning when we got there. It was a lovely, bright, almost summer day, and Malin jumped from my lap onto the soft, green grass.

'Oh, this is wonderful! Thank you for bringing me, Lily.' Malin rolled around on the grass, stretching and rubbing her face in the dirt.

"Malin, you're going to get filthy." Gwen walked around the car and crossed her arms.

'Magical being you know, you don't have to bathe me.' I giggled, and she got to her paws. *'Show me where we need to go.'*

"Yes, ma'am." I started walking down the trail, and she leapt up onto my shoulder.

'This is a nice forest,' I felt her turning her head, looking and smelling everything in the air.

"It can be really nice sometimes. Not after it rains, though. They have to close the trails down so they can dry out."

'*Ugh, rain.*' I chuckled and walked to the same tree, and Malin leapt to the ground. '*Okay, I'll summon a fae. Hopefully, they won't take long. I don't want to miss that patch of sun that falls onto your couch, Gwen. It's simply perfect.*' I smiled and turned back to Gwen, who was shaking her head at her familiar. We watched as Malin rubbed against the tree and then sat down. '*That's it, now we wait.*'

"Thank you for that." I sat down facing the tree, and Malin quickly jumped in my lap.

'*No problem. Anything to help a witch who is familiar-less.*'

Gwen sat next to me and scratched Malin's head. "Can I ask you something?"

I nodded. "Yeah, anything." She cleared her throat, and I could tell, even with my permission, she was nervous.

"You didn't know that The Order was in Arion?" Hearing someone else talk about that horrible group made my stomach flip. Knowing they were real and could be anywhere made my skin crawl.

I took a few calming breaths. I really didn't want her to realize they scared me. "I didn't, no. Jackson seemed to realize, though. Wish he told me. Might have been more prepared." I had read through his notes but still didn't find a reason he believed they were in Arion. But Jackson was a smart guy, and I told him what the Sluagh said about how The Order had summoned it. I didn't understand what that meant at the time, but clearly he did.

"Did you know about them beforehand?"

I petted Malin's head, and it helped calm me down. "You know the usual rumors, nothing concrete. Remember the boob drawing in my witchy room?" She nodded with a smile. "Jackson died before we realized they were here, and he tried to warn me through another spell. Hell, he tried to warn me in my apartment by yelling at me, but maybe something The Order did made it harder for him. I could barely hear him, even with a lit candle. The next day, we started looking for the Fells, I had cast a locate spell, and Jackson managed to use that left-over energy and made this poof of smoke above my cauldron. The smoke looked like that picture to tell me it was The Order. I, however, didn't see it, Richard did, so he drew that. The boob is a mountain."

She laughed loudly at that. "I suppose I can see that."

'I can tell you love this Richard a great deal.' My eyes went wide as Malin outed me in front of Gwen. Her head zipped to me when she heard that, her mouth open in shock. 'His scent is all over you.'

"Malin!" I looked down at her, but she clearly had no idea what she had just done.

"Really?" Gwen's shocked face turned into a smile. "I knew he had feelings for you, but I wasn't sure if you were together or not."

I looked up, still in shock. "How did you know that?" She started to answer, but the tree trunk began to open, and we both got to our feet, Malin standing regally in front of us. She was the one who summed the fae, after all. The same female fae stepped through and kneeled to Malin.

"It's been a while since a familiar summoned me," she scratched Malin's chin before looking up at us. "Ah, the new witch in town. What is your name?"

Gwen seemed startled that the fae acknowledged her. "Oh, it's Gwen."

The fae nodded. "What can I do for you?" She stood straight and clasped her hands together, looking between us.

"Thank you for coming," I gave her a little bow. "I believe I found out what Eldora is planning."

Her eyebrows rose slightly at that. "Do tell."

I cleared my throat as Malin jumped back up on my shoulder. "She was using Olin to kill three lovers to create a Calamaris."

The fae gasped, and I knew I wouldn't have to explain any further. "My, why didn't I think of that." She started pacing back and forth. "I believe you could be right."

"We found the shifter she had bound to her."

She stopped and looked at us. "You did? Is he free of the enchantment?"

"He is, so she'll have to start over. Hopefully, we'll find her before she finds another victim."

She nodded and started pacing again. "Well done."

"I take it your guards haven't been successful in finding her?"

She shook her head. "No, not as of yet, but with this new information, I'll make sure their efforts are tripled." She reached into a hidden pocket in her dried daisy dress and pulled out two acorns. "For if you find her." She handed one to me and one to Gwen. "I shall report what you've found." She started to turn back to the tree but stopped. "How did you come up with such a scenario?"

"I was reading books from some friends who had passed. They always had the best books, and I started to wonder why a fae would use a man in mourning for her dirty work. Suddenly, one of their books started to glow. The glowing page was the spell, a mourning heart killing three in love, creating the Calamaris. We discovered Eldora was in love with her victim's brother, who died a few months ago."

The fae woman sighed. "I had heard she had another mortal lover, but not that he died. I should have known. Just another piece of the puzzle we were missing. Thank you for your hard work." She started to turn again.

"Wait!" She stopped and turned to me. "I am sorry I haven't asked before, but what is your name?"

"That's all right. It's not like I offered it. It's Ostea."

I gave her a little nod. "Thank you for your help, Ostea."

She gave us a little bow and disappeared through the tree once more. *'Well, wasn't she just lovely?'* Malin jumped down from my shoulder and started walking back to Gwen's car. *'Come! The sun is almost to my favorite spot!'* Gwen and I chuckled as we put our acorns in our pockets.

"That was nice of her to give us these," Gwen said as she pulled her keys from her pocket.

"I think they really want to keep the negative aspect of this fae under wraps. Which I understand, it makes it easier for us if they're looking harder."

"You don't think we'll actually run into her, do you?" I could hear she was nervous about that. Hell, I was too. An older fae who was desperate enough to call a creature from the pits is always something to be wary of.

I shrugged, trying to stay calm. "Who knows, me more than you probably." Which was how I wanted it. As much faith as I had in Gwen, I didn't want Eldora to target her. We climbed into her car, and Malin took her place on my lap.

Gwen pulled onto the main road. "I visited Olin last night to see how he was doing."

"Oh? How is he?" We still hadn't heard if he was going to be taken into custody or not. That could be a good thing.

"Still free of that spell, thankfully. Luan and a few others in the pack were still there with him. He wanted me to help him get his memories back, but I told him it was best not to, not yet anyway. At least he didn't argue with that."

I nodded and looked out the window at the forest zooming past us. "He seems like a level headed guy."

"He does. He said when this is all over, if we need any yard work, he'd do it for free." I chuckled and petted Malin.

"Making connections, all right." My phone buzzed, and I took it out of my pocket. Malin grumbled as I had to jiggle her out of the way a bit. It was a text from Nicola.

'I looked at Faolán's autopsy report —' "Who's Faolán?" I wondered out loud.

"Olin's wife," Gwen said confidently.

"Oh! Of course it is." I had forgotten I asked her to look into that. *'I looked at Faolán's autopsy report. It was one I didn't do. Her family requested someone who had some experience in shifters, so her body was taken to Silver Springs.'* Silver Springs was a town fifty miles away to the north and was where Faolán was from. I was surprised people in town didn't send more bodies that way because of that, but now they didn't have to. *'There was a high concentration of silver in her bloodstream but also no smoke in her lungs, which to me says she was dead before the fire started. Unsure if Olin knows this or not.'*

"Oh damn."

"Hmm?" I told Gwen what Nicola told me.

"I knew he had been trying to get someone to listen to him about her death. He never believed she would die in a fire."

Gwen blew out a breath. "Doesn't sound like he knows, does it?"

"It does not." I quickly texted Nicola back, asking if Olin had ever gotten a copy of her report. She texted back that her family had blocked that request several times.

"Ugh," Gwen exclaimed. "Families always complicate

things. Should we tell him?"

I tapped my foot a few times. "Let's wait until all this is resolved." Gwen nodded as she pulled into her driveway. Malin leapt from my lap and through the cat door on the front door.

"Well, I hope she finds her ray of sunshine."

———

The two of us walked back to our desks in the precinct and saw our partners talking when I remembered that Malin ratted me out.

"Oh, uh," Gwen stopped and turned to me. "Maybe don't repeat what Malin said to anyone?"

She tried hard not to smile at that. "I won't."

"Thanks." We sat at our respective desks, and Richard walked over to his.

"Find her?" He sat down in his chair. It squeaked like it usually did.

"Yes, her name is Ostea, and she gave me and Gwen an acorn if Eldora shows up. Thankfully, she thought my theory was correct and was going to triple her efforts in finding Eldora."

His shoulders relaxed a bit. "Good, on both accounts."

"Lily?" I turned to Gwen, who was looking through some papers Hyde had just given her. "Look at this." I got up and made my way over, and so did Richard. I peered over her shoulder and saw a picture that was at least five years old. "Recognize him?" She pointed to a man standing at the back of what looked like a family picture. You know the type, everyone wears the same color shirt, standing in someone's backyard.

"Oh shit, that's Glass." He looked younger, but I could tell it was him.

"Know who that is?" Gwen pointed to a young woman to the right side of the gathering.

"Um, looks vaguely familiar."

"That's Fiona Whitlock," Hyde said.

"Oh fuck, that's the woman who killed herself?" Now, I recognized the young woman who was kissing her girlfriend's cheek as they held up an axe trophy.

"Yep." He crossed his arms, and I stood straight and watched him point to another woman in the picture. "And that is Nyla Branch."

"Are you shitting me?" Richard leaned forward and took the picture off the desk. "The woman who killed Dimitri?"

"One in the same."

I couldn't stop the stunned look on my face if I wanted to. "They were family?"

"Glass is Nyla's cousin," Hyde said. "And Fiona is her stepsister. All their last names are different, so it took a little more digging to find that connection."

"That's…insane." It was the only word I could think of at this realization.

"Isn't it? So, I'm wondering if this is just plain old revenge this fae has going on." Hyde sounded pretty confident in his theory. Honestly, I hoped he was right. Revenge was a lot easier to deal with than a creature summoned from the pits who could rip souls out of the living.

I looked up at Richard. "I sure hope so cause the alternative is frightening."

"We should let the rest of the family know to keep a lookout." Richard looked over at Hyde. "Hopefully, someone will find Eldora before she decides to kill someone else."

"On it." Hyde gave us a nod and went back to his desk.

"We should up the protection we have on our homes," I looked at Gwen, and she nodded. "Just in case."

———

That night, I took some quartz from my witchy room and placed them around my apartment. I lit the candle on the living room table and cast a protection spell that retreated into the crystals.

"What'll that do?" Richard asked from the kitchen. He was making spaghetti bolognese, and while I'm sure it wouldn't hold a candle to Intermezzos, I knew I'd love it. There was garlic bread in the oven, and my apartment smelled amazing.

"When I activate the crystals, whoever is surrounded by them won't be able to move out of the circle they'll make." I already had a spell on the door that should wake us if someone breaks in, but that's for everyday burglars, not necessarily magical ones. But I trusted it as a first line of defense.

"Handy." I went into the bedroom and got two necklaces off my little necklace tree and walked back into my witchy room. "You're a busy little witch tonight."

I smiled at his tease. "Yeah, I need to make sure everything is safe. I should do the same for your house."

"Sounds good to me." I put some frankincense resin in my mortar and snapped my fingers, lighting it on fire. It was a small piece, so it didn't stay on fire for long. My arm broke out in goosebumps, and I saw Will standing outside the door.

"Evening." I smiled at him and started looking for some mugwort leaves.

"Hello, my bonny Hen." I put the leaves on top of what was left of the resin and started crushing them together. I noticed Will didn't move, and I looked up. He was just leaning on the doorframe, his arms crossed, watching me.

"What are you up to?" He shook his head, his eyes still on me. "Want to help?" His smile grew as he walked in and leaned against the old morgue table.

"What can I get for ya?"

"Can you get me the cedar?" I pointed up at the little clear jar I had above the fresh herbs.

"Have you replaced me as your Igor?" Richard called out from the kitchen.

I laughed. "Just while you cook."

Will handed me the little cedar tube. "Look out now, Dickey-boy. I'll replace you soon enough."

I snorted and put the little leaves in the pestle. "You wish, can you get me some bay leaves?" Will walked back over to the herb jars, and I watched as he searched.

"Seems you're out, my bonny Hen." He picked up a little empty jar.

"Damn it." I walked into the kitchen and ran my hands along the spices in a cabinet next to the stove.

Richard chuckled. "What are you looking for?"

"Bay leaves."

"Up top." I looked at the top of the spice rack and saw the little container.

"Ah, there you are." I got one of the leaves out and gave Richard's backside a healthy smack, which made him laugh as I walked back to my witchy room. "Found some." I put the leaf in the pestle and ground them all up, and snapped my fingers once again, lighting it all on fire. As the smoke rose, I held the necklaces over it and cast another spell. I wanted these charms to help us keep our minds in case Eldora came calling. It was the same thing I did for Olin's duck necklace. When the magic snapped in place, I put mine on and felt the magic surrounding me. I breathed a little sigh of relief and walked back to the kitchen.

"Smells good." I leaned on the counter next to him as he

melted some cream cheese into the sauce. He put a little on the wooden spoon and blew on it as he moved it to my lips.

"How's it taste?" I blew on the spoon and took a little bite. The tomatoes were tangy, but the cream cheese cut it deliciously.

"Mm, good." He smiled and went back to stirring. "This is for you." I held out the necklace. It was a silver chain with a little ceramic peace sign. "I know it's probably not your style, but it'll keep Eldora from messing with your mind."

"Then I shall wear it with pride." He leaned down, and I put it over his head and kissed his forehead.

"Thank you."

Dinner was amazing. I swear I could taste the love he put into his food, and he could have given the chef at Intermezzo's a run for their money.

After the dishes were in the dishwasher, I walked into the bedroom. "I need to take a shower. Want to join me?" My back was to him as I lifted my shirt over my head. I didn't even hear him move as his hands were on me before I threw my shirt on the floor. I laughed as he kissed my neck, his hands pressing me against him.

"Sounds good," he whispered, and I turned to him. I hooked my finger in his belt loop and pulled him towards the bathroom. "Mm, have I ever told you," he kicked the door shut behind him. "How much I love your breasts?" One hand ran up my torso and cupped my breast as his fingers gently pinched my nipple. "How soft they are in my hand, and the lovely noises you make when I do this."

He took one of my nipples in his mouth, and I gasped at the sensation. "Oh, do you?" He nodded as I undid his belt and pushed his pants down. "Have I told you how I love that glorious dick of yours?"

He laughed and kissed my neck. "No, you have not." I gripped him through his boxer briefs, and he moaned, his eyes burning into mine.

"I love that all I have to do is this," I gave him a gentle squeeze, and he moaned into the crick of my neck. "And you're mine."

He chuckled and pushed my pants down. "Ever fuck in a shower?" His voice was quiet, and I bit my lower lip. God, how could he be so sexy?

"Nope," I said, smiling.

"We're gonna remedy that right fucking now." I laughed and turned the water on. As I bent forward, I felt him pull my underwear down my legs and heard him do the same. But I stayed bent over, testing the water, and he stepped up behind me. I could feel the heat of him against my skin and sighed as he gripped my hips.

"Sorry, it takes a while to heat up." I teased him, moving my ass a little against him.

He sighed as his hand ran down my bare back. "Oh, I know, don't even worry about it." I felt his hand slide around my hip, and his finger found my clit. I gasped as he circled it, pressing himself into me. I had never had that done to me while standing, and my legs were protesting. I moaned as I put a leg up on the lip of the tub and stood straight. My left arm reached up and laid on the back of his neck.

"Holy shit." I breathed as my hips moved in time with his finger.

"Want me to check the water?" He whispered.

"Don't you dare fucking stop." He laughed as he kissed my neck, and I felt that wonderful pressure building in me.

"You're close, aren't you?" I moaned in response. "I can

tell, your hips always jerk when you're close, and I can feel you get wetter." Those words out of his mouth sent me over the edge, and I pressed against him as my orgasm crashed through me. He held me up as my legs decided to betray me. He kissed my neck as I settled, and I turned in his arms.

"Water's probably good now." He laughed and kissed me, and we stepped into the tub. I pulled up the button, and the shower rained down on us. I turned into his chest, letting the warm water beat on my back. "Good?"

"Yes." He leaned down and kissed me. His tongue slipped into my mouth, tasting me as I sucked on him, loving every second of it.

When he finally came up for air, I kissed his chest. "So, how are we going to do this?"

He turned me so the water was beating down on him now. "Put your foot up here." He tapped the edge of the tub with his own foot, and I did as he said. His lips were next to my ear. "Now, lean down." Just the sound of his voice made me shiver, and I bent over. His hand ran along my back. "Ready?"

I melted, actually fucking melted. "Fuck yes." He stepped closer, and I felt as he slowly pushed himself in me. I don't think he'd ever gone so slow before. It was a different kind of delicious torture.

He groaned as he put himself in all the way and stopped. "I will never get tired of the way you feel around me." I smiled, but whatever I was going to say was gone as he started moving. The angle was completely different. It felt like he went deeper, like he was thicker. His hands gripped my hips, helping me to stay up as he rubbed the hidden spot in me perfectly. Every pass over that spot made me cry out, the absolute pleasure that radiated through me. My legs and arms were shaking, and I felt his hands hold onto me harder.

"Oh my god, that's amazing." I managed to say before he slowed his pace. "Oh, you're evil." He went slow. It was a constant assault on my nerves. I couldn't tell if he was moving in or out. It was just never-ending pleasure.

"Fuck, Lily, you feel so good." His hand ran over my back, but I could barely feel it because of what his dick was doing to me. I could feel my orgasm building, and I put my hand on my leg. "You're close, aren't you, Sweetheart."

"Yeah," I breathed out, and my hips jerked in his hands. "Please, pl—" Pleasure spread through me like a flash, and I cried out. It happened again, and Richard moaned above me.

"Oh fuck." He pushed himself in as far as he could go and shuddered. "Oh god, Lily." His breath trembled as he pulled me up against his chest. His hand made little circles on my stomach while the other cupped my breast, his thumb running over my hard nipple. I could feel his heart beating against my back, and I smiled.

"Damn, boy."

He chuckled, I turned, and his arms wrapped around me. "Are you okay?"

I smiled. "Never better." He helped me wash my hair, and I ran the soap all over him like I usually did. We dried each other off and got dressed for bed. Richard put on a pair of pajama bottoms, and I put on a long, silky nightgown. We snuggled under the covers, and I laid my head on his chest.

"I love you."

His hand ran along my back. "I love you too, Sweetheart." I smiled and closed my eyes, thanking my lucky stars that we had found each other.

CHAPTER 10

"Wake up, Hen!" Cold hands shook me, and I opened my eyes to see Will over me, and he looked scared. "There's a fae here, and she don't look friendly."

"What? The spell on my door—"

He shook his head. "She busted through it, Hen."

I turned and shook Richard. "Get up, Eldora is here!" He sat up like a bolt and reached for his sidearm next to the bed but stopped. My hand grasped the charm around my neck and made sure that spell to keep my mind my own was still there, and it was. A little glint of light caught my eye, and I saw Richard's charm was on the bed. The chain was broken. "Shit."

"Hen, get up!" I looked back at Richard, and he was on his feet. I hadn't even heard him move. "Move now!"

"Shit, shit, shit." I got out of bed and backed away as Richard slowly walked around the bed. His eyes narrowed as they met mine. They were full of hate. I'd never seen him like that, and my heart felt like it was breaking. But this wasn't him. It would never be him. "Richard, listen to me. You can fight this!"

"Look out, Hen!" I heard Will yell before Richard stomped towards me, his hands reaching for me.

"*Duratus!*" I waved my hand, and he stopped an inch away from me. I laid my hand on his cheek and felt that same bond that was in Olin. "No, no, no, no." Getting rid of that spell took too much time, and I couldn't do it with her in the apartment at the same time. Which meant only one thing, I had to get rid of her myself. "Fuck." I picked up my phone and texted Gwen and Hyde, hoping they were awake. *Eldora is here! Get help!* I grabbed the acorn that Ostea gave me and smashed it on the floor. I prayed that whoever was listening would hurry.

I held out my hands, summoning ice to cover them, and walked into the living room. Right by the door was a female fae. She was tall, her black hair was limp around her head, and her white dress was covered in little rips. Her eyes looked like they'd never seen a day of happiness. She had dark bags under her eyes, and her cheeks were gaunt. I had never seen a fae so shrouded in grief before. I could almost feel her heartache. Will started throwing random stuff around the apartment at her. But with a lazy wave of her hand, every projectile missed.

"Your ghost is annoying." Her voice was soft and would have been comforting if she weren't trying to kill me and hurt Richard.

"Haud yer wheesht you cow!" He yelled and stood next to me.

Her eyes burned into mine. "You took my tool from me. I know it was you who broke my connection with Olin. His soul held so much heartache, he understood!" She screeched, and goosebumps broke out over my body. "He was perfect for our revenge!"

"Eldora, I presume." I threw an ice-covered hand towards her, but a mere look was all it took before it melted around me. "Fuck."

"There's nothing you can do, little witch." The way she sounded, I almost believed her. "You cannot beat me." Fuck, she was right, wasn't she? My hands dropped to my sides. "That man will help me finish my revenge." There was nothing I could do to help Richard. I felt a tear roll down my cheek. "And after that, he will be mine." But he was mine. I wanted him.

"Wake up Hen, you know she's lyin!" I felt Will's cold hand on my cheek, and it shook me out of my stupor. That bitch was trying to bewitch me! She couldn't take my mind, but she could sure as hell mess with my emotions.

"Wanna bet?" I pointed at the crystals around the room. They lifted from where they sat, and I hoped she wouldn't notice. It was just another spell I might be readying after all. No need to pay attention to the crystals levitating around the room.

"I could not stop such things from happening, neither can you. You should have left his brother alone. He wanted them dead just as much as I did!" She yelled as her fingers poked at her chest.

"No one grieves by killing people!"

She growled and pointed at my bedroom. "Get her!" She yelled, and a ripple of magic made me shiver, and I felt the spell I put on Richard break.

"Fuck." I turned and saw he was stalking towards me once again. If I froze him again, I'd have to let go of the crystals, and then she'd definitely notice them. "Richard, please fight this!" As he reached for me, I felt a cold wind behind me.

"No, you don't!" I watched as Will walked into Richard, and he stopped. He took a few deep breaths, his eyes boring into mine.

"Richard?"

I watched as he turned to Eldora and pointed at her. "You're in trouble now, lassie." I gasped at the Scottish accent from his mouth. Will had possessed Richard to keep him from attacking me. The fae's eyes went wide as Richard/Will stalked towards her now. "You tried to hurt my Hen, now you're gonna pay!" He grabbed her wrist, and she tried another spell, but the pain from him grabbing her distracted her.

"Let me go you beast!" She slashed her sharp nails down his chest, but he didn't move. Richard/Will pushed the fae to the ground, grabbing her other wrist so tight she couldn't concentrate on anything. "Let me go, or I'll make sure you never come back!" She screamed as he held both of her wrists in one hand. I walked over and flicked my wrist. The crystals floated towards us. She flinched as the crystals made a thunk on the wooden floor, forming a circle around her.

"Whatever's in this circle will stay until I say so." I willed the crystals to light. "You weren't invited." Powerful fae or no, I didn't want her here, and the crystals should keep her there until someone arrived. Richard/Will let go of her wrist, and her arms fell to the floor. She reached out, but the energy of the crystals shocked her, and she recoiled.

"This will not hold me forever," she hissed at me.

"I don't need it to," I hissed back.

Richard/Will walked over to me, and his hand wrapped around my arm. "You okay, Hen?"

"Better than you come here." I pulled him towards the bathroom and put some alcohol on a washcloth. I wiped the blood off his chest and pressed the cloth to him, hoping the slashes would stop bleeding. "Does that hurt?"

"No," he reached up and pressed the cloth to his chest. "Just stings a bit." Fuck me, he sounded sexy with that accent. I shook my head and willed my libido to chill the hell out. He lifted my chin so he could look at me. "Are you all right?" Richard's voice with that accent almost set me on fire.

"Yeah, I'm fine, I'm good. Can you get out of him now?"

He shook his head. "No, he's still under her spell. It's not safe."

"Damn it." I heard something rattle in the living room, and we both ran to see what it was. I was hoping it was the fae coming to get her, but of course, I wasn't that lucky. Eldora had a leg sticking out of the circle, and I saw one of the crystals rolling on the floor. Before I could even get a word out, she thrust her hand in my direction, and I felt myself fly across the room. I really didn't think she'd do that. Touching the crystals should have shocked her on her ass. Clearly, I miscalculated.

I slammed into my witchy room door, and the little windows broke as I crashed into them. A scream tore from my lips as I felt the glass cut my back before I hit the floor, landing on my knees. Pain ripped through me, now I was pissed. I grabbed the back of my head to make sure it wasn't bleeding. "You did not just fucking air yeet me like some bad horror movie!" I looked up to see Eldora standing in front of a frozen Richard/Will, who was down on his knees.

"I can freeze, too." She stalked over to me and, with an invisible hand, lifted me in the air until my toes were barely touching the ground. I felt hands around my arms, invisible fingers digging into my skin. I tried to keep the whimper of pain from fleeing my lips, but I failed. I tried to kick but could barely move. "Now, your man will be my tool for revenge."

"He doesn't have a broken heart!" I screamed. I could feel blood dripping down my back and legs. She stepped closer, and I felt those arms tighten around me. The smell of dead flowers and graveyard dirt filled my nose.

"Not yet."

"Don't you fucking touch her!" Richard/Will yelled. My eyes darted over to him. He was shaking, trying to move like I was.

"Why, what are you going to do?" She whirled on him and kicked him in the side. "You're a ghost! Trapped like a parasite!" I flinched as she slapped his face. Her nails left little cuts in his cheek. "And you'll be mine soon anyway." I closed my eyes and tried to concentrate. She was in my house, at the mercy of my magic. There had to be something I could do. I pictured the big candle on my table and managed to snap my fingers. It lit up, and I opened my eyes to see a tall flame. Eldora was looming over Richard/Will, and I willed the flame to jump from the candle to her, just like I did with the Sluagh. I watched as the flame flew through the air and landed on her shoulder.

She shrieked, and that moment of panic was enough that I fell to the floor. I did my best not to land using my right hand. I won't lie. I was a little worried about my shoulder. I looked up and watched Richard/Will wrap his arms around her and slam her to the floor with a roar as I clenched my fist, putting the fire out. Her head bounced off the hardwood, and it stunned her. I ran to my witchy room and pulled a long ribbon out of a basket that I kept random junk in. I slid over to them, glass flying out of the way, and slammed the ribbon on her chest.

"*Gravis!*" She groaned as the ribbon pressed down on her. "Let's see her lift a thousand pounds." I got up on my knees, and Richard/Will did the same. We watched as she struggled under the ribbon but was unable to get out from under it.

"Impressive Hen."

"Thanks." The wall next to Eldora began to split, *fucking finally*, I thought.

Eldora gasped. "No, I deserve my revenge, Dimitri deserves it!" She kicked her feet against the floor, but she couldn't move.

"I don't think Dimitri wanted you to enslave his brother

just so he'd have somewhere to go." Ostea stepped through the wall, as did a few elven guards. We both got to our feet and moved out of the way as they surrounded her, pointing sharp spears at her. I felt Richard/Will's hands around my arms, his thumbs rubbing my skin.

"You all right, Hen?" He whispered by my ear.

"Yeah, I am now." I stepped back and put my arms around him, watching the elves.

"Eldora, you are accused of putting a bond on an unwilling shifter and of killing mortals to make a Calamaris. We are here to take you back and will determine your fate."

Her rage-filled face turned to confusion. "Calamaris? No! I was killing those related to that bitch who killed Dimitri. They let her drive drunk that night! They took my love from me with their actions, so I took theirs!"

"Seriously?" I felt my shoulders relax. She wasn't trying to steal another man's life or summon some kind of creature. It was just plain old revenge. Hyde was right. I owed him a cheeseburger. "You could have left Olin alone for that!"

She scoffed. "I knew Olin would be an easy target to fulfill my need. A heart in mourning is easily manipulated."

Ostea looked over at me. "It was a good guess."

"I feel much better knowing that all this was just revenge." One of the guards waved his hand, and a stack of papers appeared, floating in the air.

"This is for your human law." She motioned to the papers, and they floated to my side table. "Proof of what she did and the innocence of the shifter and human she used. We will take her now." Ostea touched the ribbon, and the guards picked her up by the arms. She didn't dare fight them. She was insane, not stupid.

"Thank you for all your help," I called out.

She nodded at us. "Thank you for yours."

"Hey, mind getting that spell off him?" I pointed at Richard/Will, but Eldora just sneered.

"Do it yourself, Witch!" They dragged her through the crack in the wall, and when it was sealed up behind them, I turned into Richard/Will's chest.

"Oh my god." His arms went around me, and that odd familiar feeling once again hit me, as did the knowledge that if I remembered whatever it was, it'd make me cry.

Richard/Will rubbed my back. "You all right, Hen?"

I nodded, rubbing my forehead on his chest. "Yeah, but I doubt I'll get much sleep tonight." I looked up, and he put a hand on my cheek. "Can you help me get that spell out of him?"

He nodded. "Aye, I think so." I took a breath and laid my hands on his chest and started the spell. The bond was deep in him, but nothing would keep me from getting it out of him.

"Richard, I know you can hear me. You have to think of happy things. That'll help me get you free of this." The bond was breaking, but it was slow going.

"Remember the first time you saw her," Will said. "What were ya thinkin'? I bet ye were thinkin' what's this beautiful woman doing here? I hope I can get to know her." The spell started coming apart like melted butter. I couldn't believe it. "Isn't Lily the bonniest lass you ever saw?" The end of the spell was in sight, and I felt his arms around me. I looked up into his eyes, and whatever my mind didn't want me to remember was right there, daring me to remember. "Because she's the most bonny lass I ever saw." I watched as he leaned down to my lips.

A word flew through my lips before I could stop it. "*Leannan.*" I felt a tear roll down my cheek as my heart broke.

"*Mo Bhean.*" I felt his lips on mine a moment before the

spell broke. Something bright kept my eyes closed as Richard deepened the kiss, his tongue sweeping into my mouth, and I met it enthusiastically. My broken heart was healed, and while I remembered being heartbroken a moment ago, my mind hid the reason from me once again.

When we finally came up for air, I knew it was him. "Are you all right?" I laid my hand on his cheek, marred by three deep scratches

"I'm fine, are you all right? I'm so sorry. I would never hurt you." His eyes roamed over me as his hands searched for wounds.

I quieted him with a kiss. "I know, everything's fine now."

Loud knocks on my door made me jump. "Arion police department, Ms. Roa, are you in there?"

"Yeah! One sec." I felt like I was on autopilot as I walked over and unlocked the door before remembering that I was in a nightgown. That Richard was in pajama pants and no shirt, and oh shit, he's not supposed to be here. But the door was open now, bye-bye secret.

"Come on in." I stepped aside, and everyone walked in.

"Oh, Sweetheart!" Richard quickly walked over to me, and I felt his hands on my back.

"Oh damn, I forgot." I looked back and saw the nightgown was ripped and bloody, and there was blood down the back of my legs.

"You need a medic." Major Ryan walked in and was front and center, along with a handful of other officers behind him.

"Detective," Ryan said. "Did I hear you say Roa needed a medic?"

"I'll be fine." I put my hand on my back and pushed some healing magic into my skin. I guess I was hurt worse than

I thought since I quickly relaxed at the relief I felt. I moved my right arm, making sure my shoulder didn't feel any worse, and I was glad to find it hadn't sustained any damage.

"What happened? Gwen and Hyde said you were in trouble." Richard quickly grabbed my robe and tossed it to me. I slipped my arms in it as I made my way over to the couch as officers searched the apartment. Two crime scene techs went over to the broken door and started taking pictures.

I sat down, thankfully not sore. "Our fae suspect broke in. Thankfully, Will woke me up."

Ryan seemed surprised at that. "The ghost?" I nodded. "He's here now?"

"Yeah," I shrugged, "keeps him off the streets." Ryan chuckled and nodded. "Anyway, she enthralled Moss like she did with Olin, but me and Will were able to keep her distracted until Ostea showed up with some guards and took her away." No need for them to know he had possessed Richard. They'd probably always wonder if it was really him from now on. Don't need a complication like that. A medic came in and started treating Richard's cuts while one checked out my back. I watched as Ryan picked up the stack of papers off the side table.

"That's the evidence that proves Eldora's guilty," Richard pointed at the papers in the Major's hands. "Glass should be exonerated, and Olin should not be arrested." I was impressed at Richard's ability to be calm while standing in nothing but pajama pants in an apartment where he shouldn't be wearing only pj pants. Ryan riffled through them a moment when Gwen and Hyde came in.

"Lily, are you okay?" Gwen sat next to me and gave me a hug.

"Yeah, I'm fine, we're fine. We got her."

She sat back and held my hands. "Good." I looked at Richard, who was talking with Hyde.

"Thank you for getting help."

She gave me a little smile and patted my hands. "Anytime." I watched the crime tech guys search for prints. I told them they'd be mostly on the floor, which they were. Gwen made me and Richard some tea, and Hyde kept the others at bay, letting us drink it in peace while Ryan sat in one of my chairs and read the papers the fae left us. After an hour of answering questions and pictures being taken of my apartment, everyone started to leave.

"Moss, Roa." Ryan shook the stack of papers. "This should be good enough to get all our suspects exonerated."

"Good, neither of them deserves to be in jail." I felt Richard lay his hand on my back.

Ryan cleared his throat. "Why don't you two stop by my office in the morning. We need to have a discussion." He didn't sound angry, but my heart felt like it was about to fly out of my chest.

"We'll be there, Major." Richard shook his hand, and all the other officers left with him, but Gwen and Hyde stayed behind.

"How you holding up?" Hyde stood next to the couch. I looked back and saw the glass was all cleaned up. Only one of the little windows still had glass in it. Guess I wasn't getting my deposit back. Richard was sitting next to me on the couch, his arm around me.

"Could be worse, I guess. Glad everything is going to work out for the poor guys who got messed up in this."

"You need anything? Food, drink, watchdog?" Gwen teased, and I smiled.

"No, I think we're okay, thanks." Richard turned to me

and kissed my forehead, letting his lips linger on my skin.

"Okay, well, we'll leave you two alone. Don't hesitate to call if you need something."

She squeezed my hands again. "I won't." Richard finally took his lips from my forehead and shook Hyde's hand before showing them out. When the door closed, I sat back, pulling my robe in tight. "I think we're in trouble." My breath was surprisingly shaky.

Richard sat next to me and kissed my cheek. "No, I think we're okay. He didn't tell me to leave."

I snorted and shook my head. "That's none of his business anyway." I looked around but didn't see my ghostly watchdog. I was surprised he didn't take the opportunity to throw things at Ryan now that he had no say about where he lived. "Will?"

"I think…" I looked back at Richard. He seemed hesitant as he reached out and held my hand. His eyes almost reminded me of when he told me Howard died.

"What?"

"I think Will moved on." My eyes went wide, and I felt my heart break a little.

"What? What makes you think that?" I kept looking around, and I pushed out a little magic and didn't feel him anywhere nearby. "Will?" His magic didn't answer me, and I felt a little tear roll down my cheek. "He's gone?" My lip quivered as I looked around, not wanting to believe I'd never see him again.

I felt Richard's hand on my cheek as he turned my head back to him. "He told me he was ready, that you were in good hands with me."

I shook my head. He didn't even say goodbye. "But—" That bright light when Richard was kissing me. It was Will. "No." I closed my eyes and cast one more spell to find Will, but there was nothing. "I didn't get to say goodbye." I did my best not to cry that another of my friends was gone. Not that he didn't deserve rest, but I told him once that I was selfish and didn't want him to go. Richard put an arm around me, and I laid my head on his shoulder. "Do you remember anything when he was possessing you?"

He seemed to think about it for a moment as his lips kissed my head. "A bit. I could tell he loved you a great deal." I closed my eyes, and tears finally ran down my cheeks. "I told him I'd look after you, make you happy." I covered my eyes and sobbed. How could I have lost another friend? I'd never hear him call me 'my bonny hen' again. I'd never feel his cold hand on me or talk about the goings on in the town, and I felt my heart break all over again.

———

The next morning, we sat in Ryan's office. I swore Richard could hear my heart beating out of my chest. The fact that I barely got any sleep last night didn't help, either.

Richard leaned over and whispered. "It'll be okay." I turned and faced him. I really wanted to believe him. But I also didn't want to be responsible for Richard losing his job or mine. Ryan walked in and shut the door behind him before sitting down at his desk.

"So, good work with the fae. I gave copies of the report to the judge. He isn't going to seek charges against Olin." I sighed with relief. "And I think with all the evidence you've gathered, Glass won't have much jail time. You did good."

"Thank you, Major," Richard said. I was glad he was talking because I felt like I would throw up if I opened my mouth.

"Roa?" My eyes moved over to Ryan. "You okay?"

I cleared my throat. "Um, Will moved on last night. I miss

him."

His eyes softened. "Oh. I'm sorry for your loss." I gave him a nod of acknowledgment and swallowed the growing lump in my throat. He sounded sincere, but I couldn't help but wonder if he was secretly glad the ghost wouldn't come back and make a mess of the bullpen anymore. Ryan sighed and laced his fingers on his desk. "I've had a few questions about your relationship and if that's something we need to discuss."

"Question away, Major." I managed to nod. That was all he was going to get out of me for a while.

"Do you think you can keep it professional at work? Like you have been?" I sat straight as he said that. That didn't sound like something you'd say if you were about to fire someone.

"Absolutely," I said that a little too fast. "We can be professional."

"Good. Because I think you two are invaluable to our department." He pointed at us. "Plus, you're good for each other. Especially after all the little shits you've dated in the past, Roa."

My eyebrows went up as I heard Richard snicker quietly. "What do you know about who I dated?"

Ryan gave me a little crooked smile. "I thought you grew up in this small town?"

I sat back and crossed my arms. "Touché."

He chuckled a little. "Keep it professional at work, and we shouldn't have any issues. I'll make sure no one higher up gives a shit. Okay?"

"Deal." I looked up at Richard, and he gave me a little wink.

"Good. Now go home and relax. You deserve it." We stood, and Richard shook his hand, and we walked back to our desks. There was a bottle of champagne on his desk with a note.

He lifted up one side of the little card tied to it. "Congrats on the catch. Hyde and Gwen," he read.

"That's nice of them." I practically melted into my chair. The relief was palpable. They wouldn't fire us, wouldn't make us break up (as if they could), and everything would be fine. It honestly seemed that Ryan didn't care if we were together, and I hoped that would mean he'd have our backs if, down the line, his bosses started making a fuss. Richard smiled at me as he set the champagne down.

His cell phone dinged, and he checked his texts. "I'll be right back, then we can head home."

"Okay." I watched him walk away, and I swiveled in my chair a moment before I saw Gwen walk out of the elevator.

She waved and made her way over to me. "How are you doing?" She asked as she leaned against my desk.

"Could be worse, could be better." I shrugged and noticed my right shoulder was rising higher than before. Huzzah, therapy was working.

"I'm so sorry about Will." I texted her before we finally went to bed. It was almost one am, but she texted back anyway, asking if there was anything she could do. I appreciated that even if there was nothing anyone could do. I texted Nicola as well, and it took a lot of convincing to keep her where she was and not come over. I told her I had Richard and that I'd be fine. She said she'd miss Will too, and that made the tears fall again.

I took a deep breath. "Me too. I'm going to miss him." I watched Gwen bite her lower lip like she knew something. "What?"

I could see the hesitation in her eyes. "I was wondering if I should say anything…"

I tapped her leg with my foot. "You can tell me anything."

She swallowed and scooted a little closer. "When Hyde and I brought tacos that night," I nodded. "You asked what I saw." I thought for a moment, then remembered that funny look on her face when she was holding her necklace.

"Oh yeah, I forgot about that. What was it?"

"At first, I saw a golden thread connecting you and Moss, then I concentrated a bit, and I saw that same thread connecting you, Moss, *and* Will." I remembered she looked like the cat who caught the canary, but we were interrupted before I could ask her what she was looking at.

"A golden thread?" I thought I knew what spell she was talking about, but I had never cast it before. That thread showed love. If there was no thread, I'd be completely bummed out. But I knew Richard loved me, and I loved him more than anyone, so I shouldn't have been afraid to cast it on the two of us.

She nodded. "I was being nosey, and I thought you and Moss might be together but keeping it a secret. Seems all I had to do was wait for Malin to say something," I chuckled. "But I cast that spell, and when I saw that thread, I had hoped you were together because it was clear you loved each other."

"We do." I did my best to keep my lip from quivering. "What about that line from Will?" Richard told me he could tell that Will loved me, but I was under the impression that this particular spell only worked on the living.

"I think…well, you know how ghosts are just energy, they're not actually souls?" I nodded. "I think Richard is Will reborn. You just happened to come across both of them in his life." I looked down, hoping no one was looking at us. Gwen laid a hand on my shoulder. "I mean, think about it, how he called you his 'bonny Hen' all the time and would tease you."

I reached up and touched my cheek. "Kiss my cheek." I

managed to look up. "After he found out that his brother killed him, he changed. But it was like he remembered more than what he was telling me. He'd sit on the other side of the room and just look at me. He never did that before." I could feel a lump growing in my throat. I thought back to the moment before he left, I had called him *Leannan,* and somehow, I knew that meant 'darling.' I had called Will 'darling' before he kissed me. The word had flowed flawlessly from me in the moment, like it was something I always did. I quickly got out my phone and looked up what *'Mo Bhean'* meant. When the words flashed on the little screen, I couldn't help but gasp. "Oh." I suddenly understood what my mind kept trying to get me to forget and why I felt so heartbroken. "Follow me." I got up and dashed to the elevator, Gwen following as I went down to the morgue. I saw Nicola at her desk. Thankfully, Laurette was on night duty, so she wasn't there.

Nicola looked up and gave me a sad smile. "How ya doing, luv?" I walked over and sat in the chair next to her desk, and Gwen leaned against it.

"I didn't want to burst into tears up there."

Nicola leaned forward and laid a hand on my shoulder. "Why would you burst into tears?" I bit my lip to keep exactly that from happening.

Thankfully, Gwen spoke up, so I didn't have to. "I told her I thought Richard was Will reborn."

Nicola's jaw dropped as she looked between us. "Holy shit." I sat, hugging myself, while Gwen told her about the golden thread.

"Before he left, I called him *'Leannan,'* it means 'darling.'" I saw Nicola's eyes go wide. "I don't know any Gaelic. It just...fell out. Right before he kissed me —"

"He kissed you!" Nicola leaned forward, her jaw slack with shock.

"Forgot to mention he had possessed Richard at the time. Eldora put a spell on him like she did with Olin, and Will possessed him so he wouldn't hurt me."

She sat back, still in shock. "Holy shit, he saved you."

I nodded. "He did. Before he kissed me, he called me '*Mo Bhean*.'"

I held up my phone so they could see what it meant. "Oh my god." Nicola leaned forward and hugged me while Gwen covered her mouth in shock. "How does that make you feel?"

"Heartbroken...and a little selfish." I hit the button on my phone, and the screen went dark. "I want them both."

"You have them both," Gwen laid a hand on my shoulder, and I looked up at her. "It's just all wrapped up in one hunky package this time."

I chuckled. "I suppose so. But Will was my friend." I wiped my cheeks and sat back. "I'm tired of losing friends." I looked and pointed at both of them. "Neither of you are allowed to leave."

"I'm not going anywhere," Nicola said with a smile.

Gwen shook her head. "Me either. I like it here."

The elevator door opened, and Richard stepped out. "There you are you okay? Ready to go home?"

I nodded and got to my feet. "Yeah, want to pick up a treat from Mabon's?"

He walked over and dared a kiss on my forehead. "Took the words right out of my mouth."

———

An hour later, we walked into Richard's house. I didn't feel like looking into a corner and missing Will. He set the carrier with our drinks and banana bread on the dining room table, and I set the champagne next to it.

"Is this the kind that needs to be chilled?" I read around the label, but it didn't say. Champagne was something I had little experience with, but I still wanted it to be good.

"Maybe?" Richard picked it up and put it in his fridge. "That'll work." I snickered and sat down. He walked back to me and ran his hand over my hair. "You still look like there's a million things on your mind."

"There are." He handed me a slice of banana bread, and my stomach rumbled.

"Is breakfast one of them?" He teased.

"Maybe."

He pulled out the chair next to me and sat down. "You missing Will?" He rubbed my leg, and I nodded. "I'm sorry he's gone."

I took a bite of bread. It was perfectly warm and nutty. "Well, he's not…" I swallowed my bite. "Completely gone."

"Really?" I put my bread down and took his hands. Richard looked at me, his eyes were curious, and I gave his hands a kiss.

"I love you, you know that, right?"

He smiled and kissed my lips. "I do. You know I love you, yes?"

I nodded. "I just…want you to remember that when I tell you this…kind of odd thing." He chuckled and paid attention. "Remember that night we had cheap Mexican food at my place with Gwen and Hyde?" He nodded. "Well, Gwen thought we might be together and wanted to know for sure, so she cast a spell."

He looked mildly impressed at that. "A spell would tell

her that?"

"That one, yes, but it showed her more than what she had planned on." I raised my hand and cast the same spell. To see love, and there it was, just like she said. A bright, solid, golden thread connecting our hearts. I laid my hand on his temple and let him see what I did. He looked around for a moment, then gasped when he saw the thread.

"What is it?" He reached out to touch it, his fingers hovered over it.

"Love. It shows that our hearts are connected."

He smiled, looking down at the thread. "It's beautiful. But," he looked back up at me, "what did you mean that Will isn't completely gone?" He laid his hand on my cheek, and his thumb ran along my skin.

I turned and gave his thumb a little kiss. "When Gwen cast that spell, she saw our thread but also saw one going from Will to me and you."

Confusion flashed on his handsome face. "What? Well, I guess that's to be expected, I know he loved you."

I couldn't help but chuckle at how cute he was. "Yes, he did, but this spell is generally only for the living."

He nodded. "Okay, what does that mean for Will?"

I laid my hand on his cheek. "Gwen was under the impression that you *are* Will. Reborn. We just happened to run into one of your past lives in this one."

He sat back, stunned. "Huh." I could tell he was thinking it over, but props to him for not immediately freaking out.

I reached out and laid my hand on his. "Do you remember what he called me before he left?"

He raised my hand to his lips and laid a kiss on the back of my hand as he thought. "*Mo Bhean*?" I pulled out my phone and showed him what it meant. "My wife," he whispered and looked up at me. He leaned forward and laid a hand on my cheek. "Holy shit. Our souls are connected?"

I nodded and gave his palm a kiss. "They are. We have loved each other before."

His lips parted a bit. "Soul mates?"

I nodded. "Seems that way."

His shocked expression turned to pure joy. "Really?" The way he smiled made my heart speed up.

"Really." I laid my hand on his cheek and canceled the spell. "Are you okay?" He nodded but didn't say anything. "I didn't want to freak you out, but I felt you should know."

He reached up and cupped my cheek. "Even if you freak me out, I love you. It won't change how I feel about you. It's just something that happens when you're in love with a beautiful witch. You know, again."

I chuckled. "Well, I hope I won't freak you out a lot. I'm not sure how much I want to tug on that soulmate thing." I joked.

"You tug as hard as you need to," he wrapped his arms around me and pulled me into his lap. "I'm not going anywhere, Sweetheart."

I laid my head in the crook of his neck. "Let's find a house together."

He nodded and kissed my forehead. "Good idea."

CHAPTER 11

A week later me, Richard, Gwen, and Hyde were at the cemetery with Olin. He said he was going to visit his wife and brother and wanted to know if we'd like to come with him. Gwen and I brought flowers for both their graves and cast spells, so they'd always grow and be fresh. Luan and a few members of the pack also came. I couldn't help but notice how nervous Gwen suddenly got around the tall shifter. She was quick to shake his hand, and I could tell she was trying hard not to stare at him.

"I want to thank you for all you did." Olin stood before his wife's grave, his head bowed, and his hands clasped together. "I wouldn't be free without you. And who knows what she might have made me do."

"Anytime." I patted his arm.

He turned to us. "I also wanted to thank you for getting my wife's autopsy report. I've been trying since she died, but her family kept denying the request." He shook his head, and I saw determination in his eyes. "I knew she would have gotten out of the house in time." The day after we had our talk with Ryan, Gwen and I figured it would be time for Olin to know the truth. So, the two of us hand-delivered the report to him at his house. He didn't cry like we thought he might, but he seemed more resolved than ever to find out what happened to her.

"Did your wife have any enemies that you know of?" Hyde, always the cop.

He shook his head, his arms crossing over his chest. "No enemies, but her family didn't want us to marry."

"They're pretty influential in the shifter community in Silver Springs," Luan said. "That community isn't as…loving as ours, and they wanted her to marry someone there." I noticed how the other pack members shifted on their feet, shaking their heads. Clearly, they all had the same opinion when it came to the Silver Springs crew. Gwen looked at me, and we rolled our eyes. Twenty-first-century guys, let people marry whom they want!

Olin shook his head. "They never liked me but never gave her a good enough reason not to be with me. After we married, they were just cold towards us. But when they learned she was pregnant, things changed."

"Were they overly hostile?" Gwen shifted on her feet, her hands going to her hips.

He shook his head, rubbing the back of his neck. "No, they were nice."

Luan nodded as Hyde's face twisted into confusion. "Nice?"

Richard shrugged. "Makes sense. You want someone close, you treat them how they want to be treated. It's easier to get to them that way." I nodded.

"I don't know if I'll ever find out exactly what happened, but knowing part of the truth helps." He stepped close to us and held out his hand. "I'm honored to call you my friends."

Hyde stepped up and shook his hand, Gwen smiling at the shifter. "I'm honored to be your friend as well." I shook his hand. "If you ever want us to help find out what exactly happened, let us know. I'm sure there's something we could do."

He gave a nod. "I will. Thank you again." We watched him walk back to his car, the pack in tow, except Luan.

He stood by us, watching the rest of them. "Not many people give a shit about how a random shifter died," he looked down at us. "It speaks volumes that you'd do that for him. For us."

"It shouldn't matter what a person is," Hyde said. "Justice is for everyone."

"True." He shook our hands and started after Olin. "Oh, Miss Gwen?" Gwen looked back at him, her eyes wide. "If we have need of a witch again, might I have your number?"

"Of course!" She walked over to him as he pulled out his cell phone.

"Or if I wanted to ask you on a date?" My jaw dropped, and Richard's hand flew over my mouth to keep my squeal in. I'd have to thank him for that later.

"Date? Oh, uh, yeah, you know if you wanted to." She chuckled nervously and gave him her number, and with a wink, he joined the rest of his pack. She walked back over to me, her own jaw practically on the ground.

Hyde laughed. "Did that huge man just ask you out?"

"No." She hit his arm, but her phone dinged, and she checked her messages. She snickered. "Yes." She showed me the text. *Would you like to go out Friday night?*

"You better say yes." I pointed a stern finger at her.

"If I ever say no to him, knock some sense into me," she said as she texted him back. The pack's cars were gone, leaving us alone in the cemetery.

Hyde turned to me, his hands in his pockets. "Gwen told me about Will, I'm really sorry. I feel like it's my fault. If I didn't bring that book—"

I held up my hand, and he stopped. "If you didn't bring that book, he wouldn't have been in my apartment, and I might be dead now. Nothing is an accident. Things happen for a reason, I believe that. And he's at peace now. You don't have to apologize." He nodded, but I could tell he still felt guilty.

"Well, I have a hair appointment." Gwen linked her arm through mine as we started for our cars. "I will see you tomorrow."

"Okay, you gonna keep the purple?"

"For now." She slid into her car, and Hyde got in his, and they both drove off. I took a deep breath and looked around the cemetery. They were always peaceful to me. I never understood why people feared them.

"Ready to go home?"

I nodded. "Yeah." We got into his car, and I buckled my seat belt. "I want to show you the house I want."

He smiled and turned the engine on. "Lead the way."

Karen Thrower was born in Tulsa, OK, and still resides there with her husband, daughter, and cat. She graduated from The University of Tulsa with a BA in Deaf Education in 2005. She is a member of Oklahoma Science Fiction Writers and has served in several capacities, such as President, VP, and is currently Facebook Wizard. She has been published in various genres since 2018 and was included in the bestselling anthology 'Secret Stairs: A Tribute to Urban Legend' in 2019. Her fantasy series The Last Heir of Re'Vall was published in early 2025 and is available on Amazon, Barnes and Noble, and on the World Castle Publishing website.

www.ingramcontent.com/pod-product-compliance
Lightning Source LLC
Chambersburg PA
CBHW020946180626
46814CB00003B/953